Here's what ~~readers~~ about Bluford High:

BLUFORD HIGH

Schooled

PAUL LANGAN

Series Editor: Paul Langan

SCHOLASTIC INC.

ISBN 978-0-545-39550-2

The poem "Harlem" by Langston Hughes reprinted from *Montage of a
Dream Deferred*. Copyright © 1951. New York: Holt.

12 11 10 9 8 7 6 5 4 3 2 1   12 13 14 15 16 17/0

Printed in the U.S.A.   23

First Scholastic printing, October 2012

Chapter 1

"Lionel, can you read the poem to us?"

Lionel Shephard cringed. It was the third time Mrs. Henley, his English teacher at Bluford High School, called on him today.

First she'd asked him to define what the American Dream was. Lionel joked that it was what happened when everybody in the country was sleeping. Dontrell Neeves, his classmate and friend since second grade, laughed out loud.

"You trippin,' L," he whispered.

Mrs. Henley smiled and moved on, but she returned a few minutes later, pressing him with another question. She even circled to the back row where he sat, stopping just a few feet from his desk. Her eyes beamed through her glasses like two bright headlights focused on him.

"So, as an American citizen, Lionel, what is *your* dream?"

Lionel wanted to ask her why she was always picking on him. It had been going on since he started his freshman year a month ago. Jamar Coles, his friend from the car wash where he worked weekends, would have told her off right there in the middle of class.

"Get yo' bug-eyes outta my face."

Lionel could picture Jamar shoving a desk at her and walking out in the middle of class. Of course, Jamar had dropped out of high school last year. Lionel often thought of doing that, but he knew his dad would never allow it. Neither would Mom, though she was sitting in a sandy army base on the other side of the world, too far away to do anything about it if he did.

"Basketball. I'm gonna play in the NBA one day," Lionel answered. He meant it, though half the class snickered at him.

"Yeah, me too. We all gonna play," said Rasheed Watkins from the far corner of the room. A few other students giggled.

"Why you gotta say that?" cut in Malika Shaw from the front row. "People said I wouldn't run hurdles again after I broke my ankle, but they were wrong. I'm still running."

"Whatever," Rasheed said, rolling his eyes. "He's dreamin' if he thinks he's gonna play in the NBA. Maybe smokin' something too."

"Man, I'll smoke you on the court right now," Lionel shot back.

What did Rasheed know? He wasn't there when Lionel's squad at the Greene Street Police Athletic League won the summer basketball tournament. Lionel had blocked a shot in the final seconds, allowing Greene Street to defeat the Tanner Street Titans for the first time in three years. Officer Hodden, his coach, was so happy that he'd lifted Lionel up in the middle of the court.

"You're a smart player, Lionel. Keep playin' like that and you might have a future in the sport," he'd said. It was one of the few times Lionel could remember anyone calling him smart. On the court, it was true. But school was a different story.

"Lionel? Can you read the poem to us?" Mrs. Henley repeated, snapping him from his thoughts.

Why wouldn't she just skip him? He

could handle that, coasting in the back row, working in small groups and copying what other kids did, getting them to do the work for him. He'd been doing it for years. Hadn't she realized what his middle school teachers knew, that he wasn't the one to call on in class?

"Which poem?" Lionel asked, sitting up in his desk. He knew class was almost over.

Rasheed rolled his eyes and sucked his teeth. "I told you he's dreamin', Mrs. Henley," he said.

"Rasheed, I am about to be your nightmare," Lionel cut back.

"That's enough, gentlemen," Mrs. Henley said. "The poem's called 'Harlem,' by Langston Hughes. It's on page sixty-two."

Lionel reached down and dragged his heavy textbook off the floor. Reluctantly he flipped it open, his heart starting to pound. He hated being put on the spot in class. It made his temples hurt and his palms go clammy and cold. Sometimes, it even made it difficult to focus, like right now.

"What page again?"

"Boy, don't you listen?" Rasheed hissed.

"That's enough," Mrs. Henley repeated firmly, flashing Rasheed a look that silenced him. "Page sixty-two, Lionel."

Several students snickered. Lionel could feel the eyes of his classmates crawling over him, judging him. It was like the day back in fifth grade, before Mom's army unit was deployed, when he really started having trouble in school.

Then Mr. Grabowski, a substitute teacher in his science class, asked him to read aloud a passage about insects. Lionel had always been one of the weakest readers in class. For a time, he got extra help figuring out letters and sounds. And he used what he knew the day Mr. Grabowski called on him. But it didn't help with the word "mosquito."

"*M-m-moss*," he'd stammered, trying to make the letters on the page into sounds that made sense. "*Moss-quit-oh*," he had said finally, the word as meaningless as those countless tests he'd filled in with number two pencils each year.

"*Moss quit?!*" teased a girl next to him. Lionel could still hear how the beads at the ends of her braids clicked as she shook her head at him, her face twisted into a cruel smirk. At the time,

Lionel was one of the shortest kids in class. It was years before the growth spurt that made him a wiry six-footer over the summer.

"Boy, I think your brain just quit," she had mocked. The whole class erupted in laughter. Lionel's face seared with embarrassment.

"I think you should quit talking 'cause your breath stink," he snapped back.

"At least I ain't like you—too stupid for school," she had said before Mr. Grabowski settled them down.

Though it happened years ago, Lionel remembered the moment as if it was yesterday. One ugly word from that day still echoed in his head whenever teachers tried to push him.

Stupid.

He heard it now with Mrs. Henley leaning toward him. Maybe it was true. Lionel felt that way whenever he struggled with reading and writing.

It started back in elementary school with him always being behind his peers. But it got worse in middle school, especially after Mom left.

At the time, his teachers seemed to feel sorry for him. They said nothing when he withdrew to the back of the room with the other kids who hated school. They didn't yell as much when his homework was late or when he acted up in class. It was as if they knew that Dad was struggling to raise him and his little sister Kendra, and they didn't want to trouble him.

Lionel expected Bluford High School would be more of the same, but he was wrong. Mrs. Henley and his other teachers were constantly on his case, especially today.

"I'll read it, Mrs. Henley," said Malika from her corner seat in the second row. She glanced over at him, her hair pulled back behind her head, making her curls spill like coppery ribbons down her neck. She was someone who always answered Mrs. Henley's questions. Sometimes she seemed to bail Lionel out when he didn't have an answer.

Lionel hoped Mrs. Henley would give up on him and let Malika read.

"No, thank you, Malika. We know what your voice sounds like. I want to hear Lionel's for once," Mrs. Henley said. "Go on, Lionel."

Lionel glanced down at the open page. Words covered just half of it, so he knew the poem was short. And he'd heard Mrs. Henley say the title, so he knew what the first word was. But what about the rest?

"Why do we have to read a poem anyway?" he asked.

It's what he often did when teachers tried to get in his face: distract them, push back, waste time. But this time, he meant it. Reading out loud wasn't going to bring Mom home or allow Dad to work less or stop the bullets that killed his neighbor's grandson in his neighborhood a couple of years ago.

"It's not like this or any poem really matters when you step out of this school, Mrs. Henley," Lionel continued. "I mean maybe it matters somewhere, but not here."

Mrs. Henley nodded thoughtfully.

"That's deep, yo," Dontrell said.

"I think you and Langston Hughes might have more in common than you think, Lionel," she said with a knowing grin. "Why don't you read it and we'll see."

The class grew silent again. Lionel saw Malika looking at him. Rasheed too.

Lionel could feel tiny drops of sweat gathering on his forehead. His heart started to pound. His legs bounced nervously. He took a deep breath and looked at the words, at the first letters. He tried to focus on them, figure them out. But in his mind he could hear how childish he would sound. He could feel the embarrassment already, the laughter that was sure to rain down on him. His hands curled into fists.

Ring!

The bell signaling the end of first period blared loudly overhead. Lionel sighed with relief and closed his eyes as the class exploded into chaos. Students jumped from their desks and rushed to the hallway. He slammed his book shut and made his way toward the doorway when he heard Mrs. Henley call out behind him.

"We'll have to continue this on Monday," she announced. "Lionel, can you come here for a second please?"

Lionel cringed. Why couldn't she just leave him alone? He dragged himself to her desk on the other side of the room, looking back once to see Malika disappear down the hallway.

"I gotta go to my next class," he said.

"I know, but I just want to give you this," she said, handing him a crisp white envelope.

"What is it?"

"A letter for your parents."

"For what?!"

"Because you barely participate in class. You never handed in your first assignment, and on your last quiz you scored a 50," she explained. "I think you're capable of more, and I want your parents to know it."

"Why you gotta be like that, Mrs. Henley?" Lionel asked, thinking of how upset Dad would be to see the note. "I didn't do nothin' wrong today."

"No you didn't, but that doesn't change what I just said. I want to see you focus on your work, and I think this letter can help. It's only the first marking period. You still have time to change how this class is going, but you need to start working now, and your parents need to know that."

Lionel rolled his eyes. Dad said the same thing when Lionel announced his plan to join the NBA the night his team won the Police Athletic League tournament.

"You can keep messin' around on the court all you want," Dad had said. *"But I want to see you spend some more time worrying about school. You're getting older, and it's time you start takin' your*

education seriously."

Lionel hated Dad's words. *Messing around on the court.* It was an insult, as if he was playing a kid's game, not something serious.

"Why you gotta talk about it like that? I can make more money playin' ball than I'll ever make in school," Lionel had tried to explain.

"Yeah, Dad!" his little sister Kendra had cheered. *"Then he can buy us a new house like on that show Phat Cribs. We could have a pool and four cars and—"*

"That's enough, baby."

"He's really good, Leroy. You should see how quick he is," Aunt Mimi had chimed in, bouncing her daughter, Sahara, on her knee. Aunt Mimi was Dad's younger sister. She moved in to help out right after Mom left. When Lionel started seventh grade, she announced she was pregnant, and her boyfriend was going to marry her. But that never happened.

"Yeah, I know he's quick, Mimi, but there are a hundred quick kids a block from here. How many of 'em make it to the NBA?"

Aunt Mimi didn't answer.

"Whatever," Lionel had grumbled.

"Don't you whatever me, boy. I'm try-ing to talk some sense into you. School is your ticket out of here, not basketball. Understand?" his father had said, point-ing his arm toward the barred front window that faced Cypress Street.

Lionel knew what was out there. Down the block was Kwik Cash, where strangers wandered in at all hours to sell stuff for money. Almost everything there was stolen. Further down was Dis-count Liquors and Tez's Lounge, a neighborhood bar with graffiti-stained stucco walls that smelled of urine. The area was dangerous, especially after dark. Some nights, gunshots cracked and popped in the distance.

"But Dad, if I go pro, we can move—"

"Enough, Lionel! What happens if you don't make it, huh? What happens if you get hurt? You'll just be another kid with-out an education or a future. Maybe you wind up in jail. Maybe worse. I can't have that. You understand?"

Lionel shrugged, struggling not to argue with his father.

"Yeah, I understand, Dad. But you don't," he'd added under his breath.

Now Mrs. Henley was trying to tell him the same thing.

"Okay, Mrs. Henley, I'll take the note to him," Lionel lied. He knew he'd toss the letter in the trash as soon as he left the classroom. It wouldn't be the first time.

"Good," Mrs. Henley replied. "And one last thing, Lionel. I want you to have your dad sign it. Bring it back on Monday and be ready to read your poem to the class."

Chapter 2

"Man, Mrs. Henley is really gettin' on my nerves," Lionel complained at lunch, holding the sealed white envelope in his hands. "It ain't right that she always pickin' on me."

"She like that with everybody," Dontrell said, inspecting the spongy chicken patty on his plate. "I'm about to ask if I can switch classes or somethin'."

"They won't let you," said Desmond Hodden, one of the other guys at their lunch table. Everyone called him Dez. Lionel met him over the summer at the Police Athletic League. His uncle was Lionel's coach.

"And even if they do, you might end up with Mr. Mitchell. My brother had him last year and says he's even worse," Desmond added. Lionel knew Desmond was talking about Cooper, his older brother, a popular junior at Bluford.

"Yeah, well I ain't gonna make it to next year if this keeps up," Lionel muttered.

"Why didn't you just read that poem?" Desmond suggested. "I mean, I know it's wack but maybe she'd stop buggin' you."

Lionel shrugged and took a bite of his chicken patty. He couldn't tell Desmond the truth, that when he read, he sounded like a second grader. If they heard him read, the whole freshman class would never stop teasing him. There was no way he would let that happen.

"Man, why should he?" said Dontrell. "I think what you said was right, L. I ain't feelin' those poems neither," he added, looking at Lionel. "But it's not all bad. Mrs. Henley wasn't the only one watching you in class today."

"What are you talkin' about?"

"Open your eyes, bro! Didn't you see Malika lookin' at you? That girl is fine! She got that sprinter's bootie."

"You trippin', Trell!"

"I'm serious. She's been checkin' you out all week. I know 'cause I been watching her. You gotta get the digits!"

"Yeah, you gotta show her them

skills you got on the court," said Desmond, pretending to shoot an invisible ball.

"Nah, he gotta show her his moves *off* the court," Dontrell said, slapping hands with Desmond, who cackled loudly.

Lionel felt his face suddenly burn with embarrassment.

"Man, both of you shut up," he said, shaking his head and shoving another fork of soggy chicken into his mouth.

Though he didn't admit it, he'd noticed Malika too.

* * *

Lionel folded the envelope from Mrs. Henley and shoved it into his English textbook at the end of the day. It was the first time this year he was carrying a book home. He almost felt a little silly as he closed his locker.

"Don't tell me you bringin' that thing home," Dontrell teased, pointing at the textbook as they walked out the front door of Bluford. "Man, Mrs. Henley really got to you, didn't she?"

"No!" Lionel huffed. "I just needed something to carry this," he added, flipping the book open to show the envelope.

Dontrell rolled his eyes. "You gonna have your dad sign it?" he asked as they passed Ms. Spencer, Bluford's principal. She stood at her usual spot at the front doors of the school watching students exit. "You know Mrs. Henley's gonna ask you for it Monday. She don't forget nothin'."

"I know," Lionel grumbled.

He had no idea what he was going to do about Mrs. Henley's note. If Dad saw it, he'd be furious. Maybe he'd make Lionel quit his weekend job at Nye's Car Wash or prevent him from trying to join the Bluford basketball team. Tryouts were Wednesday. But if Lionel didn't show Dad the note, Mrs. Henley would be all over him. She might call home or report him to Ms. Spencer. Either way, he was in trouble.

"Whatcha gonna do, then?"

"Man, don't worry about it!" Lionel snapped in frustration. "It's *my* business, not yours, all right?"

"Yeah, whatever," Dontrell said, looking annoyed.

Without a word, they walked down the crowded sidewalk and along the high steel fence that bordered Bluford's four blacktop courts. Three of the courts were empty, but on the last one, two guys were standing at the far end face-to-face. A small group of students gathered against the fence to watch them.

Standing just outside the fence was Desmond Hodden. He was yelling something to one of the players, a tall, dark-skinned guy with thick arms and an angular face. As Lionel got closer, he could see the guy's head was shaved so close he was almost bald. He noticed something else, too. The guy had the same friendly eyes and wide jaw as Desmond, only he was bigger and much more muscular. Lionel knew right away it had to be Cooper, Desmond's older brother.

"All right, Coop, let's do this," said the other player on the court, a stocky onyx-eyed guy with tight cornrows. He bounced the ball twice, his blue Bluford Football T-shirt stretching tight across his chest. "You may be able to handle your little brother, but there's no way you're ready to step to me."

"That's Steve Morris," Dontrell whispered. "He plays varsity football and basketball. I heard he got college scouts watching him for both sports."

Lionel recognized the name. Steve

had scored a touchdown in Bluford's win against Zamora High School a couple of weeks ago. The whole school had talked about it as if Steve was a hero. He had no idea Steve played basketball too.

Lionel walked up to the edge of the blacktop, stopping at a gap in the fence to get a good view. Several girls stood nearby talking and giggling, their eyes on the court. One of them was Tasha Jenkins, a curvy cheerleader with cinnamon skin and a cat-like face. She held a tiny pink camera phone in her skinny fingers, aiming it toward the court.

"Check it, L," Dontrell whispered. "Tasha's filming this."

Next to Tasha was Jamee Wills, another cheerleader Lionel recognized from his lunch period. Standing behind them was an older, heavy-set girl talking on a cell phone.

"Man, don't start that trash talkin' with me, Morris," said Cooper. "We both know your game ain't as fast as your mouth."

The older girl smiled. "C'mon Coop!" she cheered. "Show him how we roll so we can get outta here. We gotta go pick up my cousin, remember?"

Cooper bounced the ball once to Steve,

who bounced it back, checking it into play. Then Lionel watched as the two exploded into a half-court game as rough as a boxing match.

Cooper was fast, dribbling in, trying to push through and around Steve. But each turn he had with the ball ended in a jump shot with Steve right in his face. Cooper sank a few, but Steve scored more. He could jump higher than Cooper, and he was a half second faster with each move. Steve's last basket came when Cooper appeared to have him cornered at the baseline. Suddenly, he spun off Cooper and with a burst of speed, raced toward the basket, making an incredible leap. Lionel watched as he sailed through the air, jamming the ball through the hoop in a thunderous dunk.

Whoomp!

Cooper sank his head in defeat.

"That's what I'm talkin' about!" Steve boomed. The ball slowly bounced toward where Dontrell and Lionel were standing.

"You better hit the weights, Coop, 'cause yo' game is weak," Steve bragged. Lionel had seen guys like him all summer. Most of the time, he could beat them.

"All right, Morris, I gotta go. Good

game," Cooper said, slapping Steve's hand. "I let you have this one. C'mon, Dez."

Desmond walked over and picked up the ball. He seemed insulted that his older brother lost. Then his eyes met Lionel's, and a smile spread across his face.

"Yo, Coop, this is the Lionel that Uncle Bruce was talkin' 'bout," Desmond said. "I bet he could take Steve. I seen him play this summer. He's off the chain."

Steve turned and glanced at Lionel. So did Cooper.

"Whatcha doin', Dez? Why you startin' trouble?" Dontrell said, glaring at Desmond.

"Man, Coop, you got your little brother sending freshman at me? That's messed up," Steve said, stepping closer and flexing his hands as if he was about to get into a fight. Lionel could feel Steve sizing him up.

"Hey, I didn't have anything to do with it, but if he wants to play you, that's up to him," Cooper said, nodding at Lionel. "I heard he's good, though."

"C'mon, L, let's bounce. You don't wanna mess with him," Dontrell whispered, putting himself between Lionel and the court.

"Coop, don't go gettin' him in trouble. He didn't do nothin'," shouted the older girl. "Now c'mon. We outta here."

"Hold up, Tarah!" Cooper said, turning to Lionel. "I got your back. He ain't gonna do nothin' except play you. I'll make sure of that."

"Let's go," Dontrell urged. "That dude is trouble. I saw what he did to a freshman in gym class. You don't want any part of him."

Lionel knew he should walk away, but his feet wouldn't move. It was his chance to test himself against a varsity player. And there were girls watching. He didn't want to back down and look scared in front of them. Nearby, Tasha pointed her camera phone at him.

"Don't do this, L," Dontrell said, trying to hold him back, but Lionel shrugged him aside.

"What? You want some, little man?" Steve said, holding his arms out. "I hope you brought a change of clothes 'cause I'ma wipe this court up with you."

The small crowd standing along the edge of the fence grew. Lionel heard murmurs and nervous laughter. His heart started to pound like a bass drum. He turned to Dontrell.

"Hold this for me," he said, handing Dontrell his English book.

"Aw snap! He don't look scared to me, Steve," joked Cooper.

Lionel stepped through the gap in the fence and onto the blacktop. He glanced back and noticed the crowd outside of the court was growing. There might have been ten or fifteen people watching now. Even Tarah had come to the edge of the fence to watch. All eyes were on him.

Desmond tossed him the ball. Lionel bounced it down on the blacktop, checking its pressure and grip, listening to the tight *pop pop* it made when it hit the asphalt. He felt the familiar rush he always got when he was about to play. The same electric focus that helped him blot out Mom's long absence and his troubles at school. When he played, the world was simpler, a war with an end and rules that made sense. And unlike anywhere else Lionel knew, it was a place where he had power.

"You ready to get schooled?" Steve mocked.

"We'll see," Lionel said, his fingers tingling.

Lionel checked the ball hard against

Steve and dribbled forward from mid-court. He went straight at him, testing him.

Smack!

Steve reached in and jabbed the ball free from Lionel's hands, but Lionel predicted the bounce and recovered the ball.

"That all you got?" asked one of Steve's friends in the crowd.

"He's gonna own you in a minute, little man," someone else said.

"C'mon, L!" Desmond urged.

Lionel went to work then, bouncing the ball through his legs, dribbling on the left and then the right, darting forward and back. Steve guarded him carefully, adjusting quickly, faster than all the kids at PAL. But Steve was too aggressive. Lionel had an answer for that.

Lionel faked forward, shifting to his right foot and motioning his right arm as if he'd continue straight to the basket. Steve took the bait, sliding to his right, but at the last instant, Lionel crossed over to his left. Steve tried to recover but lost his footing. He slipped back on his ankles and landed on his backside straddling the foul line. Lionel pulled up with a clean look at the basket. He took a quick jump shot.

Swoosh!

"Whoa!" The small crowd hooted and hollered. Cooper doubled over in a fit of laughter as different voices shot insults at Steve.

"He just broke you down, Steve!"

"Steve, you better get an ashtray 'cause you just got smoked!"

"You just got schooled by a freshman!"

Steve glared at Lionel, jumping up from the blacktop and grabbing the ball as if it was a weapon. Lionel knew Steve was going to come back at him strong. He braced himself as Steve checked the ball hard into his chest.

"Easy, Morris," Cooper warned.

Steve dribbled right at him then. When Lionel had him stopped at the baseline, Steve pivoted, swinging his elbows wildly.

Whack!

Steve's elbow caught Lionel in the side of the jaw, snapping his head back and splitting his lip. Lionel spit blood as Steve slammed the ball behind him with a loud thunk.

"Whoops, my bad," Steve said with a smug grin.

Lionel's head rang from the impact.

He could hear Dontrell yelling something in the distance. He wiped his lip and was about to shove Steve when Cooper darted in front of him, grabbing his arms and forcing him back.

"Man, why you always playin' dirty, huh? He scored on you straight up. That don't give you the right to play rough."

"Get outta my face, Coop. I'm just teachin' him, that's all. Maybe he'll join the basketball team this year. I want him to be ready," Steve said.

Just then two school security guards in blue shirts walked up on the court, their radios crackling as if they were police officers. The small crowd immediately broke up as the guards approached.

"School's closed, which means these courts are closed, too," one of them announced. "Everybody go on home."

The other guard stared at Lionel's face.

"You okay, son?"

"Yeah, I'm fine," Lionel replied, swallowing a bit of his own blood. Steve strolled away, not once looking back.

Chapter 3

"Oh my God, did you see what he did to Steve?"

"He got skills. Mad crazy skills."

"Who *was* that?"

Lionel ignored the talk fading in the distance as he quickly walked away from Bluford High with Dontrell at his side. His lip was sore, and the metallic taste of blood lingered on his tongue.

"Man, I told you not to play against him," Dontrell said as they neared SuperFoods, the grocery store just down the block from school. "But I gotta say that move you put on him was da bomb! The whole school gonna be talkin' about that on Monday."

"Yeah, and they'll be talking about how he clocked me, too," Lionel said bitterly.

"Nah, if you ask me, you won that

one. Here, I gotta go," Dontrell said, handing Lionel his English textbook and slapping his hand. "My mom's picking up Chinese food tonight, and I'm starvin'. Later."

Lionel watched as Dontrell cut across the wide SuperFoods parking lot and headed to Union Street where he lived with his parents and little brothers. He imagined Dontrell walking in to find his family sitting at their wobbly kitchen table cluttered with containers of sweet and sour chicken and pork fried rice, his favorites. He could almost hear them talking excitedly about the things that happened to them this week. Dontrell would cackle out loud at something funny, spitting his food the way he did at lunch.

A knot of jealousy tightened in Lionel's chest. He wished Mom was home waiting for him to come in so they could eat a big dinner together. But those days were long gone. He remembered the Saturday morning in July when he learned that Mom's deployment had been extended. He'd been secretly listening to his parents' weekly talk on the phone when his father cried out from the bedroom.

"What?! A year, baby?! They gonna

keep you for another year?!" Dad moaned, and then his voice cracked and broke up, a heavy painful sound Lionel wished he'd never heard.

"How am I supposed to take care of everything without you?" he asked over and over again.

Lionel felt sick. He pretended to be asleep and never told his father that he'd heard everything. Later that day, he sat stone-faced when Dad gave him and his sister the news. Kendra wept quietly, but Lionel just stared at the floor, shrugging off his father when he went to hug him. He spent that afternoon on the PAL court, taking shots and playing anyone who would step on the court with him. Officer Hodden seemed to know he was upset and let him stay late that night without asking questions.

"I'm glad you're here and not somewhere else right now, Lionel," he'd said, watching him curiously. *"Better to use that anger on the court than on the street."*

Lionel ran for an hour up and down the bleachers, hoping to strengthen his legs to improve his vertical jump. Afterward, he tried over and over again to dunk the ball, but he just couldn't get high enough. The ball always clanked awkwardly against the rim and bounced back into the court no matter how hard he tried.

That night, Lionel sat alone in his dark bedroom, his legs shaky, his body sore from hours on the court. But the pain was nothing compared to the emptiness he felt inside at Mom's absence, an ache that throbbed again as he watched Dontrell rush off to be with his family.

"You don't know how good you got it, Trell," Lionel mumbled under his breath, heading up Cypress Street to his house. Around him, traffic cruised noisily up and down the block. Some cars sped by, leaving a trail of smoky exhaust. Others moved slowly, blasting music that rumbled the warm afternoon air with heavy bass that made Lionel's insides tremble.

Two doors from his house, Ms. Walker swept her small front porch the same way she did every day before Lionel could even dribble a basketball. On Sundays, when Lionel was a little boy, she and Mom would often sit on the stoop together after church and watch him run and play on the sidewalk, especially right after Kendra was born. Sometimes Mom would buy ice pops, and they'd all sit on the stoop and eat them together until their fingers got sticky and their tongues turned colors. Mom would tease Lionel because he was always the first to finish.

"Where'd that popsicle go?" she'd say, pointing to his stomach and tickling him until he could barely breathe.

Back then, Ms. Walker's voice was still strong, and she would use it to read books to Kendra or scold Lionel when he ran too close to the street. Once she'd even smashed her broom against the snout of an angry dog that chased Lionel right up to her porch.

"Old Ms. Walker is tougher than any dog, that's for sure," Dad joked at the time. Lionel had laughed at his father's words.

But when Lionel was in seventh grade, Ms. Walker's grandson Russell was gunned down walking home from school just a few blocks away. Even though Russell was two years older, Lionel knew him well and had nightmares for weeks after the shooting. He could still remember staying up with Dad the night Russell died and hearing Ms. Walker wailing next door.

"My baby's gone!" she cried over and over again. *"They took my baby!"*

Ms. Walker was never the same after that. Her smile was gone forever that day. Her once friendly eyes became stormy and impatient. Even the jerky way her broom scratched and clawed the cement steps seemed raw and bitter somehow. Lionel never knew what to say to her anymore. At times, it almost seemed she was resentful when she saw him walking by. Most days, he hoped to avoid her, but he couldn't do that now.

"Hi, Ms. Walker," he said weakly, eyeing his house just a few feet away.

She stopped sweeping and glared at him as if he'd just done something wrong.

"Why's your lip so swollen?"

"I got hit at school playing basketball. No big deal," he said, wishing she'd stop staring at him.

Ms. Walker shook her head disapprovingly. "Your momma comin' home anytime soon?" she asked with an edge to her voice. "I think you and your dad could use her."

"Nah," Lionel replied, realizing that she probably didn't know Mom's tour had been extended. "Not for another year," he said.

"Another year?" Ms. Walker huffed. She seemed outraged, as if what Lionel said was his fault. "That don't make any kind of sense. We got so much shootin' out here right now, they should be sending some troops into *this* neighborhood!"

Lionel nodded. He agreed with Ms. Walker, but he was hungry, and his face hurt. All he wanted to do was go home, not sit and listen to her complain about something he couldn't control. But after everything she'd been through, he couldn't just walk away. That wouldn't be right.

"Whatcha got there?" she asked, pointing at the English book in Lionel's hand. He could see her craning her neck to read the cover.

Lionel sighed. "Just some homework for English class."

Ms. Walker's eyes widened. "And you brought it home? Lionel, I've watched you for years and never seen you bring a book home from school. You in trouble or something?"

"No," Lionel blurted, cringing inside. If he could just get to his front door, he could escape Ms. Walker's nosy questions. "I just gotta study some poem about dreams or something . . . by this guy Langdon Hughes."

"You mean Langston Hughes?" Ms. Walker's voice rose as if he'd told her something important. She leaned her broom against the side of her house and turned to him. "Is the poem 'Harlem'?"

Lionel nodded impatiently. "Yeah, yeah that's it. Anyway, I just—"

"What happens to a dream deferred?" Ms. Walker interrupted, closing her eyes for a second as if she was recalling a distant memory.

"Huh?" Lionel asked, unsure how to respond.

She took a deep breath and spoke again, her voice suddenly powerful, her words rhyming, like a strange rap or chant.

What happens to a dream deferred?

Does it dry up
like a raisin in the sun?
Or fester like a sore—
And then run?
Does it stink like rotten meat?
Or crust and sugar over—
like a syrupy sweet?
Maybe it just sags
like a heavy load.

Or does it explode?

She paused several seconds then, and Lionel didn't know what to say. Maybe after everything that happened, he figured, she was starting to go a little crazy. Maybe the long nights alone in her house had gotten to her.

"I taught that poem for years, Lionel. I was a teacher, you know, long before your time," she explained. "Even taught it to Russell, God rest his soul." Her voice wavered then, and she turned away quickly.

Lionel hadn't heard her mention his name in months. And in that same instant, he realized she'd just recited the poem Mrs. Henley asked him to read. The odd rhyme that rolled off her lips was the same one he'd have to say on Monday.

Ms. Walker took her glasses off and rubbed her eyes. He could see she was struggling with memories of her grandson. For several long seconds, they were both quiet. Far off, a siren wailed into the afternoon sky.

"I'm sorry, Ms. Walker," he said finally. It was all he could think of to comfort her.

Ms. Walker grabbed her broom and began sweeping again, more forcefully than before.

"You better get home. Go on, Lionel. It's almost suppertime."

Lionel nodded and left her on the porch in a swirling cloud of memories and dust.

* * *

Inside the cluttered living room, Lionel found Aunt Mimi sitting on their old lumpy couch holding Sahara, who cried loudly, tears streaming from her dark brown eyes.

"What's wrong with her?" Lionel asked. Plastic baby toys littered the floor, and the TV was turned up loudly, showing a cartoon family singing nursery rhymes. The music made Lionel's head pound.

"She's teething," Aunt Mimi said wearily. "Been like this all day."

On weekends, she worked at Essentials, a salon where she cut women's hair and did their nails. During the week, she stayed home, taking care of Sahara and helping out around the house while his father was on the road driving an eighteen-wheeler truck for Allied Freight. Most weeks he was gone four or five days at a time, hauling loads hundreds of miles away.

Sahara whined and shoved a plastic doll in her mouth. Saliva spilled down her chin onto Aunt Mimi's lap.

"Aw c'mon, Sahara. That's nasty," Lionel complained.

"If I don't get to the store and get her some medicine, ain't none of us gonna sleep tonight," Aunt Mimi said, grabbing her purse. "I might as well do the grocery shopping while I'm at it. You think you can handle her for a while so I can go?"

After the day he had, the last thing Lionel wanted to do on a Friday night was babysit his cranky niece.

"Where is everyone?" Lionel asked. "Can't Kendra do it?"

"Kendra's goin' to the movies with friends tonight, remember? And your dad called to say he's gonna be late," Aunt Mimi explained. It was the third Friday in a row his father wasn't home on time.

"What about dinner?" Lionel protested, thinking of Dontrell again. "I'm starving."

"There's that chicken I made the other night. Just heat it up," she said moving toward the door. "So you two gonna be all right?"

Lionel rolled his eyes. He knew there

was no getting out of babysitting. And there would be no family dinner either. Just another night of leftovers while Dad was away again. He wanted to complain, but what could he say?

"Yeah," he grumbled, grabbing the remote and flipping the TV to the sports channel. Sahara stood in front of him and immediately started to cry.

"Thanks, Lionel," Aunt Mimi said studying his face for a second as she stood at the doorway. "What happened to your lip?"

"Nothing. I just bumped it on the court, that's all."

Sahara put both her hands in her mouth and flung a large glob of drool onto his shirt.

"Girl, that's gross," Lionel said as Aunt Mimi left, locking the door behind her.

Later that night, after changing two diapers, putting Sahara to bed, and eating a plate of dry leftovers in front of the TV, Lionel nodded off, his mind drifting to the court.

In his sleep, he soared high with the basketball.

Over their noisy cluttered house.

Over Bluford High School and Mrs.

Henley's questions.

Over the city with its dangerous blocks and crowded cemeteries filled with young people like Russell.

Over the cold ocean that kept him from his mother for too long.

Whoomp!

The ball slammed through the iron hoop, a perfect dream interrupted hours later when his father came home and gently led Lionel down the hall to bed.

Chapter 4

"Man, who she think she is?" said Jamar at Nye's Car Wash the next morning. Lionel had left for work without even talking to Dad, though he heard him snoring as he passed his parents' bedroom when he went to take a shower.

Lionel had just explained to Jamar everything that happened in Mrs. Henley's class. Jamar had quit school in the middle of his junior year.

"I'da been like, 'You need to get outta my face if you know what's good for you,'" Jamar added as they cleaned the inside of a silver Lexus. Felix, another worker, was carefully drying the hood.

"I almost said that to her," Lionel admitted.

"You should have," Jamar replied. "What's she know? Ain't no poem that matters when you're out here. I'll tell you what matters—this," he whispered, taking a handful of change from a compartment in the car's dashboard and sliding it into his pocket.

Lionel looked away. He hated when Jamar took money from people, but he couldn't stop him. At least he only did it to people who disrespected him or had expensive cars.

"Hey, anyone who can afford this car ain't gonna miss a little change," he'd said the last time Lionel complained. Jamar lived a few blocks away with his two older cousins. He'd moved in with them when his grandparents kicked him out for quitting school.

"I'm serious," Jamar continued. "I been out of school over a year now, and I don't miss it one bit. No more getting up early or sitting in some boring class. Now I get paid for what I do instead of wastin' my time dealing with teachers gettin' on my nerves. I'm not havin' that no more."

Jamar sounded as if he was boasting, like guys on the court who didn't have the skills to back up their words. But Lionel liked what he was saying. If he quit school, he wouldn't have to worry about Mrs. Henley, and he could play basketball whenever he wanted. Sure, he'd lose the chance to play for Bluford, but he could still play for the summer league until he was eighteen. And by then, he'd be old enough to try out for the NBA. It made sense, except there was no way Dad would allow it.

"I gotta say that sounds nice," Lionel admitted.

"So quit," Jamar suggested. "I told you before. I don't know why you still go to Bluford. What's the point?"

"I can't quit. My dad would throw me out in two seconds if I dropped out. And my mom would scream so loud I bet I could hear her from here," Lionel explained.

"So what? Let 'em yell. Check this out. If your pops kicked you out, you could stay at my crib with me and my cousins. We got room. I'm serious."

Lionel's mind was spinning. In a way, the idea was perfect. It made everything simple and easy. Dad would be mad, but so what? He was hardly home anyway. And by the time Mom got back, Lionel figured he might be playing pro basketball, making enough money so that both his parents could retire.

"Man, don't listen to his nonsense. He's just tryin' to drag you down with him," cut in Felix, wiping the outside of the car's door with a fluffy white towel. Lionel had almost forgotten he was there.

"What do you mean?" Lionel asked.

"He ain't bein' real with you, that's what I mean," Felix said. "This ain't no picnic. Trust me. I been here three years now. It's startin' to get kinda tired, you know what I'm sayin'?"

"Ain't nobody asking for your opinion," Jamar said, closing the doors of the Lexus and wiping away the smudges his fingerprints had left behind. "Me and Lionel are talking, not you."

"No, you ain't talking. You're just blowing smoke like always, and I'm calling you out," he snapped, turning to Lionel. "Look at me. I dropped out three years ago. It's been three long years, and I'm still here, working with kids like you. No disrespect, but there ain't no goin' up from here. If I could go back to school, I'd do it in a heartbeat, but I can't afford to," he said, pausing while he scrubbed a stubborn streak on the windshield.

"It's funny, when I was a kid, I

43

dreamed I'd own my own Lexus. Now I'm drying someone else's," Felix continued, shaking his head.

"Don't listen to him, L. He just mad 'cause his girlfriend's pregnant."

Lionel stepped back, shocked at the news.

"He's right," Felix said, glaring back at Jamar. "She *is* pregnant, and this job's not makin' me enough to pay the bills. I'm actually thinking of joining the army. I heard you know something about that, Lionel."

Lionel felt as if his head was about to explode. There was too much news, too many choices, too much chaos. It was like jump ball at the start of a basketball game, only there were a thousand arms fighting for the ball, and the game was meaner than anything that happened on the court. It all made Lionel dizzy. He wished he could just get away and find a quiet space where he wouldn't have to think about school, Felix's words or anything else. Instead, Felix was staring at him, waiting for a response.

"Well, whatcha think?" he asked.

Behind them, a growing line of cars stretched halfway around the block, their drivers glaring impatiently. One of them, a man in a smoky Mercedes, beeped his horn twice.

"That dude's change is mine," Jamar mumbled.

"Man, I don't know if you wanna do all that. My mom still ain't back yet," Lionel said to Felix, feeling a wave of resentment at what his home had become since she left. "How you gonna raise a kid if you ain't there?"

"C'mon guys, hurry up! This is a car wash, not a parking lot," cut in Mr. Nye, their boss.

All three of them grabbed some clean towels and rushed to the next car, letting the conversation die. But for the rest of the day, Lionel kept thinking about Jamar's advice. No matter what Felix said, the idea of quitting school was tempting. The low grades, the never-ending tests, the impatient stares from teachers, the uncomfortable feeling of being behind everyone else—all of it would finally be over.

"You really got room in your crib?" Lionel asked Jamar at the end of the day as they waited in line to get paid.

"Man, that's what I been tryin' to tell you," he replied. "C'mon, let's go there right now so you can see how we livin'."

With the sun setting overhead, Jamar led him up several blocks to 43rd Street. Then they made a left and walked up to a single-floored red house surrounded by a rusted iron fence. There was a break in the fence where a gate once stood. Its busted hinges stuck out like broken teeth in a ruined smile. Wedged against both sides of the fence were bits of trash, plastic bottles, and a grease-stained paper bag. Inside was a small yard of burnt-out grass and a single ancient rose bush spiked with thorns, as if it was trying to protect itself. Behind it sat a dented trash can half full of beer bottles and buzzing with flies.

Jamar opened the door to a blast of rap music. Lionel recognized the track, one he used to listen to before each basketball game over the summer.

Ain't wastin' time on no haters
Ain't waitin'—it's now, not later
On the court, they call me the mayor
Give me the ball, and watch me
    slay ya

"Cool. Andre's here," Jamar said. "C'mon in."

They stepped into a cluttered living room with a blotchy beige carpet. A sagging green couch sat just a few feet in front of a color TV. Next to it on the floor was an old silver boom box the size of a small suitcase. An end table held crumpled fast food wrappers stained with ketchup that looked more like dried blood. The thick scent of marijuana smoke hung in the air.

Sitting on the couch was a guy Lionel never saw before. He was focused on the screen playing NBA Slams, a video game Lionel often played in Dontrell's basement.

"What up, Andre?" said Jamar as they walked into the living room. "This is Lionel, the dude from the car wash I was telling you about. He might come stay with us."

"'Sup," Andre said, not once looking up from the screen. His fingers busily worked the controller.

"C'mon, Lionel, I'll show you where you can crash."

Lionel followed him down a scuffed hallway to a sparse bedroom that smelled even more strongly of weed. A single mattress rested on the floor in the far corner. A gray cat was curled up in the middle of the bed, but it jumped when they walked in.

"That's Smoke," Jamar said as the cat scurried away.

Unfolded clothes were scattered at the foot of the bed, though Jamar quickly scooped them up into a crumpled pile as Lionel walked around the room. A black plastic table was wedged against the mattress. On top of it was a clock radio, a cell phone charger, a short stack of magazines, and some loose change. There was also a single photograph. Lionel could see the faded image of a woman sitting on a swing holding a child on her lap.

"You'd share this room with me. Only twenty-five bucks a week. I'm hookin' you up big time," Jamar said.

Lionel nodded. He didn't know what to say. He could afford the rent if he kept working at the car wash, but did he want to live there? The house was an escape from school, but it wasn't much more.

"I don't know, Jamar—"

"C'mon, bro! I ain't sayin' this place is perfect, but you can do anything you want up in here," Jamar said, an edge to his voice. "Ain't no one gonna bother you no more about school or class or nothin'."

Lionel thought Jamar was being

pushy, but he didn't want to say that. Instead, he changed the subject.

"Who's in the picture?" he asked.

"Oh, that's me and my mom from back in the day," Jamar said, staring at the photo for several long seconds. "Ancient history."

Lionel waited for Jamar to say more, but he didn't. Instead he sighed and fished through his pile of laundry. Then he leaned over and grabbed at something under his mattress.

"You wanna get high?" he said then, opening up a small plastic bag filled with what looked like crushed, dried leaves.

Lionel tried to hide his surprise. It wasn't the first time someone offered him drugs, but he hadn't expected it from Jamar. Lionel had heard the countless warnings from his parents all his life. Officer Hodden explained how drugs could slow his brain function, meaning that Lionel's basketball skills would suffer. Lionel wanted no part of that. Besides, drugs were a line he'd promised Mom long ago he'd never cross. He wasn't about to break that promise now.

"Nah, man," Lionel replied, pretending to notice the clock. "Yo, I gotta get goin'. I told my dad I'd be back soon."

"So you gonna come stay here or what? We could use a roommate, for the rent and all," Jamar said, gently cradling the plastic bag in his palm as if it was precious.

Lionel's head was spinning again. There were just too many choices, too many decisions to make. It was like a rebound he couldn't predict.

"I gotta think about it," Lionel said, stepping into the hallway. "I'll get back to you."

"All right, but don't think too long," Jamar said, following him back into the living room where Andre was still gazing at the TV screen, the rap music pounding in the air.

Like a jet, I soar right by ya
You play forward but I rewind ya
You step up but I don't mind ya
Cause my skills take me higher

The player on the screen muscled through two defenders, leaped forward, did an impossible 360-degree spin, and dunked the ball through the hoop.

"You see that?!" Andre boomed, pointing to the screen. "Yo, Jamar, you know you can't do that!"

"Neither can you, not in real life,"

Lionel thought to himself as he stepped back into the ruined yard, more alone and confused than ever.

* * *

It was almost dark by the time Lionel reached Cypress Street. The corner lot across from Discount Liquors was crowded as Lionel rushed past, careful to ignore the many eyes that watched him. He spotted his father, standing at the front door as he neared the house.

"Lionel, where you been? You were supposed to be home an hour ago. I was about to start looking for you," his father said, eyeing him up and down as if he was inspecting him for damage. "You know these streets ain't safe at night."

"Relax, Dad. I just worked a little late, that's all," Lionel lied. There was no way he could explain to his father that he was thinking about quitting school and moving out. Lionel wondered if the smell of marijuana smoke was still on his clothes as he walked up the steps.

"Everything okay with you? School's goin' all right? Your lip looks a little swollen," his father said. He was always the same after his trips, full of questions as if he was trying to make up for being away for days at a time. But Lionel knew the attention wouldn't last. Dad would soon be back on the road and forget most of what they talked about. Lionel had seen it all a hundred times, especially about school.

"Yeah, everything's fine, Dad. I just bumped myself playing basketball. No big deal."

"I'm glad to hear you're spending less time on the court and more time on school. Ms. Walker tells me you started reading Langston Hughes. I saw your English book on the table," his father said with a smile.

Lionel cringed. He'd forgotten about the letter from Mrs. Henley. It was folded inside his textbook. Lionel glanced and saw that the book was still sitting unopened where he'd left it, just inches from his father. He could also see the envelope sticking out between the pages.

"Yeah, I have a little homework to do," Lionel said, reaching over and grabbing the book from the table. He was careful not to move too fast.

"I guess you're finally starting to take school seriously," Dad beamed.

Lionel shrugged. "I guess."

"That's the best news I heard all week. Maybe all year," his father said, putting a hand on his shoulder.

Lionel squirmed inside at his touch. He felt guilty lying to his father's face, and yet he was angry at how clueless Dad was.

"It ain't no big thing, Dad. All I did was bring a book home."

"But you never bring books home," interrupted Kendra, coming out of the kitchen with a glass of soda. "I'm the only one that does homework around here," she added.

"Not anymore," his father replied. "Maybe Lionel will be joining you on the honor roll soon. That's a dream come true."

"Yeah right," Kendra huffed.

Lionel winced. He imagined telling Dad the truth right there in the middle of the living room.

Dad, I'm sorry, but I ain't never gonna be on no honor roll. I'm thinkin' of droppin' out. But I promise I'll make you proud on the court one day. You'll see.

He pictured Dad's reaction. It would be like those bombs that blew up on roadsides near where Mom was stationed. Only this one would go off in their living room. Lionel could almost

53

hear it ticking while he sat next to Dad.

After a few minutes, he couldn't stand it anymore and rushed down the long hallway to his bedroom, closing the door behind him. Beneath the Lakers posters covering his ceiling, Lionel pulled out Mrs. Henley's envelope and carefully tore it open.

He scanned the sheet of paper, figuring out the short words and slowly sounding out the longer ones. He hated how his voice almost stuttered as he struggled with certain words, but gradually, in the quiet of his bedroom, he was able to figure out some of what Mrs. Henley wrote.

No effort.
Little focus.
Poor work.
Danger of failure.

At the bottom of the page was a long blank line where his father was to sign. He knew if he let Dad read the letter, he'd be punished. His father would take away the one thing in the world that Lionel cared about: basketball. Lionel couldn't let that happen.

He grabbed his notebook and a black pen from his nightstand and practiced writing his father's name.

Leroy Shephard.

Lionel knew his own handwriting was messy, and his spelling was so bad that he barely wrote anything in school unless it was his own name or a single word or *True* or *False*. It had been just enough to get by in the classes he'd been assigned to in middle school, especially when friends were nearby who could help him or let him copy their work. But Lionel had seen how Dad scratched his name on things. His signature was just a wavy scribble. After four tries, Lionel was satisfied that his scribbles looked like Dad's.

Then, with his palms sweaty and his moist fingers trembling, Lionel dragged the pen across Mrs. Henley's note. He forged his father's signature.

Chapter 5

On Sunday morning Lionel shifted uncomfortably in the wooden pew of Holy Faith Church, the church his family had attended for years. Reverend Simmons was talking about someone he called the prodigal son, a boy who disobeys his father and fails at everything he's been asked to do.

"Look at this young man. He's foolish. He's wasteful. Irresponsible. A failure to his family . . ." the reverend went on.

Lionel flinched, afraid that the sermon was about him. He knew it was wrong to fake Dad's signature and lie about school. Yet what choice did he have? There once was a time when he'd pray for things. But after Russell died and Mom's tour was extended, Lionel decided that God didn't listen to him.

"And yet this son is not lost. None of us are," Reverend Simmons continued.

Lionel shrank back in his pew. He felt more lost than ever. Lost in school where he couldn't keep up. Lost around Jamar who was comfortable stealing change and smoking weed. Lost to his father who wanted him to be an honor student. There was no way that could happen. It was like asking him to fly.

If only school was like basketball, Lionel thought to himself. Then he could pivot and spin, tricking his opponent into making mistakes, just as he did with Steve. He imagined himself on the court with Mrs. Henley then, trying to fool her into thinking he could read. And that's when the idea hit him, a way to get her off his back. He just needed his sister's help. He waited until they were home and Dad was playing with Sahara.

"You think you smart enough to do high school work?"

"Huh?" his sister replied suspiciously. "Why you askin' me that?"

"Last night you acted all smart. I just wondered if you could do what we do at Bluford," he said, pausing just enough to hook her. "Never mind. I know it's probably too hard for you."

He knew his sister couldn't resist the challenge. She was just like him, a competitor. If she'd played basketball, she would have challenged Steve too.

"What is it?"

Lionel took out his English textbook and opened to page sixty-two. The poem faced him like a puzzle. He'd heard Ms. Walker recite it once, and he remembered the first and last line already. If he just listened to it again, he figured he could memorize it so he could say it out loud in Mrs. Henley's class. Then she would get off his case, and he wouldn't have to read anything else.

"See if you can read this out loud," he said, handing her the book. "It's okay if you can't. I know you're just a fifth grader."

Kendra stared at the short poem for a moment and then smiled defiantly. A second later, she was reading it aloud, much better than he could. Lionel focused on her. Listening to every word. Getting her to repeat lines by telling her she stumbled. Committing each to memory as if it was his favorite rap. When she finished, Lionel was finished too. He'd learned it.

"That was easy," Kendra said proudly

when he took the book away.

"You're pretty smart," Lionel replied with a proud grin of his own.

* * *

Late Sunday afternoon, Lionel was staring at his textbook practicing the poem in his head when he heard a knock at the door. Aunt Mimi was still at work, and Lionel and Kendra were in the living room watching Sahara. Dad was in his room.

"Who's that?" Kendra asked.

"I don't know," Lionel said as he approached the door. He peeked through the tiny peephole to see a pretty woman holding a tray covered in aluminum foil. "Some lady," he said as he clicked the lock and opened the dead-bolt.

Lionel opened the storm door to see a slender woman, maybe in her forties. She wore a snug plum dress, and Lionel could smell sweet perfume in the air. He figured she was there to sell them insurance or something, but then she caught him off guard.

"Oh, you must be Lionel. You look just like your father," she said with a nervous smile. Was she wearing makeup too? Lionel wasn't sure.

"Yeah, uh, can I help you?"

"I'm sorry. I'm Denise. I . . . work with your father. Is he home?"

Just then, Lionel heard steps behind him.

"Denise! What are you doing here?" Dad asked, stepping in front of Lionel, nudging him aside. He spoke quickly, as if he was surprised and maybe a bit uncomfortable, Lionel thought.

"Well, I know you've been on the road all week, and I figured since you don't have anyone to cook for you right now, I thought I'd do it."

Lionel's eyes widened as she handed Dad the tray.

"Denise . . . you shouldn't have—"

"Now Leroy, don't say a thing until you try it. It's homemade macaroni and cheese. There's enough for everybody."

"Well, thank you," Dad said, moving into the doorway, as if he was trying to block her from coming closer. "But you didn't need to come all the way over here."

"I know. But I know how busy you are and how hard we've been working these past weeks. I just thought y'all could use a good meal. Besides, Lord knows I like to cook," she added with a smile that seemed to linger on Dad for several seconds.

One phrase echoed in Lionel's mind. *How hard we've been working.* She acted as if she and Dad had some long history. And yet Dad had never mentioned her name before. Why?

"Well, we do like to eat," Dad said, shifting uncomfortably. "Especially him." He nodded toward Lionel.

"Oh, I know how they can put it away," she said, looking at Lionel and Kendra as if they were on display. "You two got a good father. He's always talking about you and saying what good kids you are."

Lionel felt uncomfortable under the strange woman's gaze. What did she know? And why did she think they needed food, as if they were some sort of charity case or something? Worse, why did she smile at Dad that way? Would she do that if Mom were around? Lionel didn't think so.

"Can you put this in the fridge, Lionel? Kendra, why don't you help him make some room."

"But Dad, he doesn't need my help."

"Kendra!" Dad insisted, flashing her a look.

"Okay," she grumbled and followed Lionel to the kitchen.

Lionel dropped the heavy tray on the counter. It was warm and smelled delicious. The macaroni inside was golden and crisped just right. But Lionel wasn't about to eat it, not until he knew more about this strange woman who made it.

"How do you think he knows her?" Kendra asked.

"You heard them. They're just friends from work, that's all," Lionel answered, trying to hide his concern from his little sister.

By the time they'd put the food away, Denise was climbing back into her car. Dad waved weakly as she drove off.

Once she was gone, he raced back to his room and didn't mention her until Lionel asked him about her that evening at dinner.

"She's just someone I work with," Dad said quickly, between bites of macaroni and cheese. His eyes seemed focused on his plate as if he didn't want to see Lionel and Kendra's stares.

Lionel thought about Dad's answer. Part of it didn't make sense. Before he knew it, he was asking Dad another question.

"But you're on the road all week," he said. "How you spending time together if you're not even in the office?"

His father was about to take another bite, but stopped. Lionel could see his jaws tighten.

"Why do you sound like you're accusing me of something, Lionel?" Dad barked, a flash of anger in his eyes. "I told you she's my coworker. There's nothing more to discuss, you understand?"

Lionel shrugged, unsure what to believe. Waves of bitterness suddenly bubbled inside him, as if Denise's visit had opened up some deep wound.

"Seems like you see her more than you see us," he blurted. His pulse was throbbing in his neck and his hands were suddenly trembling. There was burning in his eyes too.

Dad stared at him for several seconds and then leaned back in his chair and rubbed his temples wearily.

"I'm sorry I can't be here more right now, but I'm just trying to keep us afloat. You understand?" Dad replied, a mix of sadness and hurt in his voice.

"Yeah, but I ain't floatin', Dad. I'm

sinking, and you don't even know it," Lionel thought as his father sighed, got up from the table, and stepped outside.

* * *

Lionel walked to school in a daze Monday morning. He'd barely slept after talking with Dad. Even as he rehearsed his poem for Mrs. Henley's class, Lionel could hear questions bounce through his mind about Denise.

Why had Dad hid her for so long?

How did he spend so much time with her?

Did Mom even know about her?

The questions buzzed in his head as he climbed the steps to Bluford High and nearly collided with Dontrell.

"Yo, L, wassup?" he said, slapping his hand. "I told you everybody'd be talkin' about Friday. I heard Tasha Jenkins put a video of you online."

"What?" With everything on his mind, Lionel almost forgot about his one-on-one game with Steve.

"I'm serious! She filmed you takin' Steve to school, and then she sent it to, like, fifty people on Saturday. You some kinda star right now."

"Whatever." Lionel shrugged as they walked down Bluford's crowded main corridor. He felt as if he was trying to dribble five basketballs at once and losing each of them.

"There he is!" yelled a familiar voice from behind him. "That's my boy right there."

Lionel turned back to see Cooper with a wide grin on his face. A taller boy named Hakeem Randall walked with him. Lionel recognized him from church where he used to sing in the choir. He even wrote a song for Russell when he died.

"Wassup, Coop," Lionel said.

"Yo, L, I could watch that clip everyday. Steve fallin' on his butt like that. That one had me rollin' 'cause that's just what that boy needed," Cooper said with a loud cackle. "Please tell me you're tryin' out for basketball on Wednesday."

"Yeah, I'll be there," Lionel replied, the thoughts of his father still gnawing at him.

"Cool! Maybe we'll actually win this year," Cooper said turning up a different corridor. "C'mon, Hak. Let's go before Tarah gets mad."

The two juniors walked away, and

Lionel and Dontrell snaked around a corner to their lockers. That's when Lionel saw Malika. She was huddled outside a classroom with Jamee and Tasha, whispering something. Their eyes were focused on the pink phone in Tasha's hand.

"I'm not even gonna ask what y'all are looking at," Dontrell said as soon as he saw them, a big grin on his face.

"None of your business," Tasha replied, flipping the phone shut and slipping it in her pocket. Malika looked embarrassed.

Overhead, the warning bell sounded.

"Uh oh, we don't wanna be late. Let's go," said Jamee, yanking Malika away.

"See you in class, Lionel," Malika said with a wave and a smile. As the three girls hurried down the hallway, Lionel could hear Jamee laughing and teasing her friend.

"See what I mean? Everybody's talkin' about what happened," Dontrell said with a smile. "Yo, you gotta talk to Malika today. She's waitin' for you to make a move."

"We'll see," Lionel mumbled, the questions about Dad still churning in his mind. He could feel Dontrell watching him as he dropped his coat in his locker and slammed it shut with a loud metal clunk.

"What's wrong, bro? You feeling all right?" he asked then, staring at Lionel's face as if he saw something that worried him.

The final bell rang then. Classes were starting in one minute.

"I'm cool. Just got a lot on my mind," Lionel said, shouldering his friend aside as he moved down the crowded hallway.

* * *

Two hours later, Lionel walked into English class. Mrs. Henley eyed him the second he stepped into her room.

"Do you have that letter for me?" she asked before he even sat down.

Though he was ready, he was tired of her pressuring him. She acted as if her class was the only thing he had to worry about.

"Nah, I forgot," he said, watching for a second as her face tightened up. He wished he could walk away and not have to deal with her anymore.

"Just kidding. I got it right here." Lionel carefully pulled the letter from his book and handed it over, hoping his fake signature was good enough to fool her.

Mrs. Henley glanced at it for several seconds and nodded.

"Good. And are you ready to read for us today?"

The class was beginning to fill. A noisy group of students, including Rasheed, barged into the classroom. Malika came in a few steps behind them. She glanced quickly toward Lionel's desk as soon as she walked in. When their eyes met, she smiled and darted to her seat. Seeing her, Lionel felt a nervous tremor race through his stomach.

"Yeah, I'm ready."

He had repeated the poem to himself several times since Kendra said it. He even rehearsed it during his Study Skills class as Mr. Coleman talked about the importance of taking notes. It was the closest thing he'd done to studying since he arrived at Bluford.

"Great! Let's get started so we can hear it."

Dontrell was the last to arrive in class, and he looked shocked to see Lionel with an open book on his desk.

"Now I *know* you ain't feelin' right," he whispered.

Mrs. Henley took attendance quickly and then settled the class down, reminding them of their discussion about the American Dream and what each of them had said last week. She even remembered Lionel's joke, about the country being asleep.

"Go ahead, Lionel. Read us what Langston Hughes has to say."

For an instant, Lionel's mind was blank. Sweat gathered beneath his arms, and he felt the eyes of his class-mates scanning him. Rasheed grunted and sucked his teeth. Dontrell clicked his pen. Someone nearby snapped a piece of gum. It was as if he was on the court dribbling the basketball in slow motion. And for once, he had a move he could use in the classroom.

"What happens to a dream deferred?" he said, glancing once at the page and then straight ahead. The whole poem came to him then, naturally, powerfully. Perfectly.

For a line or two, the words of Langston Hughes almost seemed like his. He knew about dreams that were held back. He'd seen them choked off everywhere, from Felix at the car wash, to Ms. Walker and poor Russell. And he had his own dream that was in danger, one he clung to as he recited each word.

"Excellent, Lionel. You read that beautifully," Mrs. Henley said when he finished the poem. Lionel's heart pounded with pride. He felt as if he had just made a game-winning last-second shot, a feeling he never had in class. For the rest of the period, he listened to Mrs. Henley's discussion. He even knew the answers to her questions, though he kept quiet, and she left him alone. But at the end of the period, she made an announcement.

"For Wednesday I want you to take all your ideas and write an essay," she said, handing out the assignment

The class groaned in protest. Lionel crossed his arms and slouched back in his seat as she described the details.

"Four pages . . .

"Use what you've read and experienced . . .

"What does the American Dream mean to you?"

Lionel shook his head in frustration. He'd done what she wanted, and now she was piling more work on. It was as if he was being punished for listening.

"The final draft will be due next Friday and count as twenty-five percent of your marking period grade. It must be handed in on time. No excuses."

Lionel crammed the assignment into his book and watched the final seconds of class tick away. There was no way he could write a four-page essay for her. His writing was as bad as his reading. Maybe worse. What was the point of trying if she was just going to fail him anyway?

Too stupid for school. The old familiar chorus echoed in his head as the bell rang.

Chapter 6

"Can you believe Mrs. Henley's giving us more homework?" said a girl's voice as he left the classroom. Lionel turned back to see Malika. He hadn't even noticed her following him because he was so upset. "It's like she forgets we have six other classes."

"I know," Lionel agreed, unsure for a second what to say to her. He never talked to girls about school, especially someone like Malika who handed in her assignments and raised her hand in class. Except for Mrs. Henley, they had nothing in common. "It's like she likes torturing us or something," he added.

Dontrell emerged from the classroom right behind them but turned away with a grin when he caught them talking. Lionel pretended not to see him.

"I think she especially likes torturing you," Malika replied as they walked down the hallway. "But that's your fault."

"Huh?"

"She can't figure you out. Sometimes you act like you hate school. Then you get all serious like today. Other times you act like you're tryin' to be funny."

"What, you don't think I'm funny?" Lionel joked, ignoring her comment about school and pretending to be hurt. He couldn't help but notice the caramel glow of her skin, the graceful curves of her hips in her jeans, the distracting way her T-shirt rested on her chest.

"You're kinda funny. Corny too, especially for a basketball player," she teased. She stared at him with her chocolate eyes, and he nearly forgot why he'd even been upset.

Lionel shook his head, feeling a bit embarrassed.

"So watcha thinka my game?" he asked, trying to tease her back. "I know y'all were watching me."

"Maybe we were, maybe we weren't," she replied, shrugging her shoulders as if she didn't know what he was talking about. She couldn't hide the glow of her smile, though he could see she tried to.

"Whatcha think? Go on, be honest."

"You're . . . okay."

"Just okay?"

"Maybe a little better than okay. Just a little, though," she said, squeezing her fingers together to make her point, a wide grin on her face.

"You think *you* can school me? Let's hit the court right now. You gotta promise not to elbow me though," he joked.

"Hey, I got some game," she replied with a look that said she was only half kidding.

"Oh, that's right, you a track star. Tasha got a film of you too? Maybe I can watch it."

"Not yet, but you watch me this spring. I'm just getting started."

"That's how I feel. Give me a few years. You'll see," he said, surprised at his own honesty as they walked further down the hallway.

"So why you wanna be a basketball player anyway? That's what you're gonna write about in your essay, right?"

Lionel cringed for a second.

"My essay?" he asked, remembering Mrs. Henley's assignment. He didn't want to lie to Malika, but he couldn't tell her the truth: that he knew he'd fail even if he handed in his best work. "We'll see. That's a long story," he said with a sigh.

"See, there you go gettin' all serious again, just like in class," she said, watching him for a few seconds as they reached a stairway and stopped. He felt as if he was a book and she was flipping through his pages. "You sure you just wanna be a basketball player?"

"*Just a basketball player?*" he asked, his head spinning at her question.

To him, the words meant everything: power and respect where there was none; an escape from the streets; a guarantee his parents could be together without worrying about money; a home with a yard where Kendra was safe and Sahara could play. That was his dream, one he couldn't write for Mrs. Henley, or explain to Malika in the middle of the hallway between classes, though part of him wanted to.

"What do you mean, *just* a basketball player?" he challenged. "What's wrong with that?"

"Nothin'." She walked away slowly but then turned back. "It's just usually, I don't like basketball players," she said with a radiant smile and raced up the steps.

Lionel felt as if she'd just dunked on him as he moved on to his next class.

* * *

For the rest of the day, Lionel's teachers picked up where Mrs. Henley left off.

In pre-algebra, Mr. Stevens gave a pop quiz, passing out a sheet with two problems on it. Lionel had always been good with numbers. For years he followed scoring totals and statistics for many NBA players, but this quiz contained word problems. Lionel had barely finished the first one before time had run out.

"Another 50," he thought to himself.

Mr. Stevens frowned as he glanced at Lionel's half-completed answer sheet before collecting the rest of the class's work. Later, in the middle of history class, Ms. Brooks called on Lionel to answer a question about ancient Egypt.

"Can you tell me what Egyptians used papyrus for?" she said.

"Yeah. They smoked it," Lionel joked.

Several students laughed, but Ms. Brooks didn't smile. She repeated her question. He had no idea what the answer was and knew if he waited long enough, she'd move on to someone else.

"Lionel?" she said again, almost as if she was mocking him.

A few hands went up. Seconds ticked by, and he could feel his anger building. Why wouldn't she just let it go? His pulse throbbed in his head, but he kept still, his eyes focused on the window. Outside, the sun was shining.

"If you'd read your homework last night, you'd know. It was used as paper for writing," she explained. "In fact, it's where our word *paper* comes from."

"So maybe they *did* smoke it," someone said, and the class snickered.

Lionel remained motionless and Ms. Brooks steered the discussion away from him. But inside he felt as if he was sinking again just as he had in his other classes. When the bell rang, Ms. Brooks told him he was going to have to sit at a desk in the front row from now on.

"It'll help you get more focused," she explained. She also warned that his poor attitude and lack of participation was going to be reflected in his grade. Lionel stared unblinking at the chalkboard as she spoke.

In his final class, physical science,

Mrs. Copeland made everyone sit in a big circle so they could do an experiment. She asked Lionel and two other students to come forward to help demonstrate something called momentum. Eric and Antoine, the other two students, stood up right away, but Lionel hesitated. He wasn't in the mood to be in front of the class with everyone staring at him.

"C'mon, Lionel. You can do this. It's easy," she said, urging him into the center of the circle. "It will only take a minute."

Lionel felt his face burn at the word easy. Maybe she didn't mean it, but it sounded to Lionel like an insult. *"Even someone stupid like you can do this, Lionel,"* she might as well have said.

Lionel decided right then that he wouldn't budge.

First, he ignored her, acting as if he hadn't heard her speaking to him, but she kept asking him, putting him on the spot.

"No, I can't do it, Mrs. Copeland," he said finally, his anger bleeding into his voice. "It's too *hard* for me."

"Excuse me?" She stepped back and turned her head to the side.

Just like on the court, he saw where

she was going, predicted her reaction, and figured out how to avoid her next move.

"I don't feel good today, Mrs. Copeland. I think it's something I ate," he replied, acting sincere. It was another trick he used since middle school. Sometimes it even seemed as if teachers were relieved to get him out of their class. "My stomach hurts. I think I need to go to the nurse."

Mrs. Copeland studied his face. He knew she was trying to figure out if he was serious. Part of him felt bad for lying, but another part wanted to get away from what he knew was coming: another nagging lecture, another pointless warning about his decline in school. He didn't need to hear it.

"Here," she said finally, handing him a hallway pass.

Minutes later, Lionel was stretched out on a smelly vinyl cot in Nurse Wilkins's office. He lay motionless as the clock ticked away the last period of the day, and his mind dreamed of a time when school would be nothing more than a memory.

* * *

After the final bell, Lionel bolted from the nurse's office and headed down the speckled gray hallway toward his locker. The halls were filled with the crash and thud of lockers being slammed shut and the voices of students rushing to get out.

But Lionel spotted something that stopped him in his tracks. The nurse's office was close to the gym, and Lionel noticed that one of the thick steel doors of the gym was partially open. The hardwood floor glowed honey-golden against the dull tiles of the hallway.

Lionel stopped and peeked inside. Long rows of navy and yellow sports banners hung proudly over the empty gym. Each was sewn with Bluford's mascot, the buccaneer, along with a symbol for the sport that had won it. The top of each banner listed the team name and year. Most of the banners were for the football team. Others were for wrestling. Only three said Bluford Basketball, and they were all old. He read the years.

1995. 1999. 2004. Since then, basketball hadn't won anything.

"Someone's gotta change that," Lionel thought to himself.

Not far from the door was a metal

rack full of basketballs. He knew he shouldn't walk in without asking. But no teachers were in sight, and he couldn't resist. The quiet court called him.

Lionel stepped onto the hardwood, feeling the smooth surface under his feet. He wished he had his good Nikes on, the ones he saved for his PAL games, as he walked over and took a ball from the rack. He bounced it, as always, feeling the grip, the air, the rock-like firmness. It was perfect.

And then he was possessed, driving to the glass of Bluford's varsity court, letting the ball roll off his fingers and sink through the bright new net, banging down shots from the baseline, nailing jumpers, short and long, with a swish as sweet as a kiss. The stress of school and home evaporated with his sweat as he worked.

"This court is closed, son. You're not supposed to be here," came a scratchy voice from somewhere behind him, snapping his concentration.

Bong!

Lionel's last shot ricocheted off the rim. He turned back to see a middle-aged man with gray streaks in his hair. He wore a short-sleeve navy blue shirt and carried a clipboard in his hand. A whistle dangled from his neck. The man walked closer as Lionel rushed to retrieve the basketball.

"I know. I-I'm sorry," Lionel stammered, putting the basketball back in the metal rack. "I just—"

"Saw the court and figured you'd take some shots?" the man asked with a knowing smile. Fine wrinkles stretched from the corners of his eyes, but otherwise he looked strong and fit.

"Yeah, I guess so." Lionel shrugged. He started walking back toward the hallway.

"I used to be the same way. Still am sometimes," the man said, wheeling the squeaky metal basketball cart into a nearby closet and closing the door.

Lionel was about to leave when the man spoke to him again.

"Think you can shoot like that in a game?"

It was one question Lionel knew the answer to.

"I know I can," he said.

The man smiled and pulled out a pen. "What's your name, son?"

"Lionel Shephard."

The man scribbled into his clipboard

and then squinted his eyes as if he was recalling a distant memory. "Did you play for Bruce Hodden in the PAL league this summer?"

Lionel nodded. "Yeah. We won the championship."

The old man smiled and shook his head. "I used to be his coach. We still talk from time to time," he said, reaching his hand out to shake Lionel's. "I'm Coach Barber. And I suggest you come to basketball tryouts on Wednesday. You won't have to sneak in here then."

"I'll be there," Lionel said, his heart pounding as he shook Coach Barber's hand.

Chapter 7

"Lionel! Quick, quick!" Aunt Mimi shouted as he approached his house. "Your mom's on the phone!"

Lionel ran the last steps to the front door and dashed into the kitchen to grab the phone. Mom usually called only on weekends, but once in a while, she'd get a window of time to use the phone and make a surprise call.

"Hi, Momma," Lionel said as soon as Kendra gave him the phone. Her eyes were blotchy and red as she handed it to him.

There was a usual delay of several seconds as his voice reached her on the other side of the world.

"Hi, baby," she said then, a sound that filled Lionel with emotion. "How are you?"

"I'm fine," he said, unsure how to

answer her question standing in the middle of the kitchen with his sister and aunt nearby. "I miss you."

The line was quiet again. He imagined her standing in a sea of sand, the sun beating down on her with relentless dry heat. The phone crackled in his ear, and there was her voice again.

"I miss you too, Lionel. You don't know how good it is to hear your voice. How's Bluford going? Kendra tells me you're reading poetry in school."

Lionel felt his face burn. Why did Kendra have to tell her about that?

"It's true," he said. "I read Langston Hughes." Even though it was a lie, he knew it would make her happy.

She cheered on the other end of the phone. Then he heard her telling someone what he just said. He could hear the pride in her voice. It scalded him like hot water, a burn of shame.

"And are you taking care of your father like we promised? I need you to do that while I'm away."

"Yeah, I'm looking out for him," Lionel said as Aunt Mimi passed in front of him and grabbed some juice from the refrigerator for Sahara. For a second, Lionel saw the aluminum tray Denise had given them. He turned away, feeling strange just looking at it. He wondered whether he should mention it to Mom, though he didn't know what he would say.

Just then there was noise on the other end of the phone, and Lionel could hear his mother talking to someone.

"Baby, I have to go, but I just want to tell you how good it is to hear your voice. Sometimes it's the only thing that keeps me going over here," she said, pausing for a second. "I can't wait to get back home and see you all again."

Lionel felt a tightness in his throat and his eyes getting moist. He turned so no one could see his face.

"Me too, Momma," he said, leaning into the wall wishing somehow he could just reach through the phone and hug her. "Be safe."

She said goodbye then. Lionel said it too, but the phone clicked and went dead before he could finish the words. She was gone.

* * *

That night at dinner, Lionel asked Aunt Mimi the question that had been on the tip of his tongue since Sunday afternoon. They were eating dinner, and Dad was away until Friday with a delivery.

"Do you know Denise?"

Aunt Mimi was cutting up a potato for Sahara, who sat in her high chair next to Lionel. Kendra was on the opposite side of the table.

"Not really. I spoke to her on the phone once or twice, that's all," she said quickly.

"She calls here?" Lionel asked, nearly dropping his fork at the news. Why hadn't anyone told him?

"Yeah, so? Lots of people call here when you're at school," she said, watching as Sahara scooped some of the potato into her mouth. "She seems nice."

"What's she want?"

"Lionel, I didn't ask her a million questions," his aunt explained, her brow wrinkling the way it always did when she got annoyed. "She asks for your father, that's all. Why? What's your problem?"

"I ain't got no problem," he huffed, careful to hide his thoughts. Aunt Mimi hadn't seen how Dad acted when Denise visited. If she had, Lionel figured she'd be as alarmed as he was. "But don't you think it's strange that she's bringing us food? It ain't like we starvin'."

"She's probably just being friendly, that's all. Nothin' wrong with that," his aunt added. "Besides, I know one thing about her: she makes a mean macaroni and cheese."

Lionel got up from the table then, not even finishing his dinner. He didn't want to argue with Aunt Mimi or worry his sister. But in his mind he could still see the way Dad looked at Denise, as if she was a secret he needed to hide. Why?

He raced into his room and crashed on the bed, staring at his Lakers poster overhead, his mind spinning with confusion. A few minutes later, he heard a knock at his door. It was Kendra.

"What's up?" he said.

"I don't know. You're makin' me think somethin's wrong. Why were you askin' so many questions?" He could see she was worried. The last time she'd come to his room looking worried was when gunshots went off in the middle of the night up the street and Dad was away.

"Just don't worry about it, Kendra. We was just talkin', that's all," he said, trying to calm her.

"I mean what's the big deal if they talk or go out once in a while?" she asked.

"Go out?"

Kendra nodded and admitted that she'd heard Dad talking on the phone and agreeing to meet Denise one Friday night two weeks ago. Lionel was stunned, his heart pounding at the news.

"Why didn't you tell me?"

"I don't know," she said, shaking her head. "I guess I didn't want to think about it. They're probably just friends, right?" Kendra asked.

Lionel could hear her question hang in the air. She wanted him to reassure her, to tell her not to worry.

"Yeah probably. I'm sure that's what it is," he said. It was the best he could do, and it seemed to work. After a few seconds, she sighed and left, leaving Lionel with a splitting headache.

He hoped he was wrong about Dad, but his gut wouldn't let him believe it. Dad going out without telling them, being late every Friday, and acting so strangely when Denise was at the door. It all pointed to one conclusion: Denise was more than a friend. Their family was coming apart, with Mom thousands of miles away.

Lionel leaned back on his mattress and gazed up at the poster hanging over his bed, a black and white snapshot of a dunk. His NBA dream. It was his only answer to the storm in his mind, his fears about Dad, and his growing troubles at school.

He thought of the assignment Mrs. Henley would be collecting in two days. There was no way he could write an essay that would pass in her class. Unless he was copying someone else's work, his writing was filled with more spelling mistakes than anything else. And four pages? How could he possibly write that much about anything?

Too stupid for school, the old voices mocked him.

But school was stupid too. Who cared about algebra and momentum and papyrus? Why did any of that matter? And yet there was the moment in English class he could not escape. It repeated in his head like a song he didn't want to remember.

"Excellent, Lionel. You read that beautifully."

That instant he connected with the words in a book, a poem about how dreams die or explode when they go unfulfilled. In that moment, school made sense, like a shot arching through the hoop. In that moment, he belonged in class with Malika and everyone else.

Lionel reached under his bed and grabbed one of the dusty notebooks Aunt Mimi bought him at the start of the school year. He turned to the first page and drew a basketball banner just like the ones hanging in the Bluford High School gym. He took his time to get the seams just right as his eyes began to get heavy.

"Lionel's dreem," he wrote underneath the picture just before he drifted off to sleep.

He was alone on the darkened court then. The Bluford gym was black except for a single spotlight that beamed down over a basket in front of him. The ball was in his hands. And he knew what he had to do. It was his turn to dunk.

He prepared his approach, dribbling around to get his feet set just right. And then he ran forward.

Three big steps.

The take off.

His vertical was better than ever. He rose and rose until his head was well over the rim and he could see the glass in front of him. Only it was a mirror. His reflection was inside it, moving in slow motion. But it wasn't alone.

Surrounding him in the darkness of the

mirror were faces staring back at him.

Dad. Russell. Ms. Walker. Jamar. And there were other figures in the background trying to muscle out of the glass but they were stuck.

Faceless, shadowy ghosts.

Using all his strength, he slammed the ball through the hoop. A thunderous dunk.

Crack.

He was falling then, but something was terribly wrong. He thought the glass behind the rim had shattered. Instead it was him. He had been in the glass and destroyed himself. Pieces were crashing down everywhere, broken bits of the world he knew. And he fell with them and in them, watching as his own legs exploded into jagged shards on the concrete. Then his stomach. His chest. His face.

Deafening blackness.

Lionel woke up covered in sweat, his heart pounding. The nightmare was gone, but the cloud of dread it left behind hung in the dark room through the long siren-filled night.

Chapter 8

Lionel felt a nervous twinge in the pit of his stomach as he approached Bluford High School Wednesday morning.

He'd been awake since 4:22, his legs twitching with nervous energy, his fingers tingling and clammy, his mind buzzing about the basketball tryouts now just hours away.

At 6:00, frustrated and restless, he got up, showered, and packed his gym bag with everything he'd need: his good Nike high tops, the baggy black army shorts Mom sent him, and his gray *Greene Street Basketball* T-shirt. During breakfast, he mentally rehearsed everything he wanted to show Coach Barber. His quickness, jump shot, ball-handling, inside game, and defense. Finally he would have his chance.

"You ready for tryouts?" Dontrell asked as they grabbed their seats in English class.

Lionel nodded, barely able to sit down he was so tense.

"Man, you ain't got nothin' to worry about, except from her," Dontrell added, nodding at Mrs. Henley, who was taking attendance. "You do your homework?"

"Nah," Lionel scoffed, pretending the assignment meant nothing to him, as if he didn't care that Mrs. Henley would take back the praise she gave him the other day.

"What about you?"

"Yeah, I wrote what it's like when you don't believe in no American Dream, kinda like that poem you read," Dontrell said, pulling several crumpled sheets of paper out of his notebook. They were covered in his messy handwriting complete with scribbles. "She probably gonna fail me, though."

Staring at Dontrell's pages, Lionel felt a stab of jealousy. It was as if he was forced to watch from the bench when he should be in the game. For once, he wished he had something to hand in, something to prove he understood what they'd been doing in class, something to make Mrs. Henley say "excellent" again, but that was impossible. All he had was a drawing that everyone would laugh at if they saw it. His frustration grew and spread like a rash.

"Man, who you trying to be, Trell?" he said with a smirk.

"Whatcha mean?" Dontrell looked puzzled.

Lionel knew he should just shut up. But his bitterness was like a poison, bubbling in his gut, spilling uncontrollably from his mouth.

"Look at you sittin' there with your homework all done like you an honor student, like you better than me or something."

"It ain't like that—"

"You think some stupid essay you write is gonna change anything? You just like me, Trell, stuck at the bottom. Ain't nothin' ever gonna change that." Lionel fumed, angry at himself.

"What's yo' problem, L? What'd I do?" Dontrell asked, a mix of hurt and confusion in his voice.

"Just forget it," Lionel said, wishing he could take the words back and walk away.

"Man, I'm just tryin' to survive up in here. Maybe what I did isn't great, but it's better than sittin' around waitin' to fail. If you ask me, *that's* stupid."

"You callin' me stupid?" Lionel snapped, exploding from his chair and glaring down at his friend. The entire class turned to face them. Mrs. Henley rose from her desk and rushed toward the back of the room.

"That's not what I meant—"

"Is there a problem here, gentlemen?" Mrs. Henley asked, moving nervously between them.

White-hot rage swirled inside Lionel. Rage at his friend whose words stung with truth, at his classmates with their essays ready to be collected, at the school where he felt lost each day, at himself for being unable to do better.

For several seconds, images flashed in his mind like scenes from a nightmare. He saw himself shoving Mrs. Henley aside, beating Dontrell down in the middle of the crowded classroom, hearing Malika scream as he landed punch after punch on his old friend. He'd show them he still had power, even if he failed in school, even if he was stupid.

But deeper inside, standing there in front of his peers, Lionel knew it was all wrong, that his anger had nothing to do with Dontrell.

"Use it on the court." Officer Hodden's advice from the summer came back to him. It was the only answer he had, the one thing that still mattered. He remembered tryouts were just hours away. The thought pulled him like a lifeline from the boiling sea of rage.

Lionel took several deep breaths. "Ain't no problems," he answered finally, grabbing his chair and slouching into his seat. "We just talkin', that's all."

Mrs. Henley and Dontrell avoided him through the remainder of class. When the bell rang, Lionel hoped to slip away quickly, but she called him just as he reached the door.

"Lionel, I didn't get a rough draft from you," she said, leafing through a thick stack of papers at her desk. "Is there a reason for that?"

He felt blood rushing to his face again.

"Reason, nah, I'm sorry, Mrs. Henley," he said with a shrug. "I thought you said it was due Friday," he added, trying his best to sound sincere. "I'll try to get it in then."

She rubbed her forehead and dropped the stack of papers into a large folder. "I'm disappointed, Lionel, especially after the letter I sent home. You can do better than this. I know it," she said with a sigh. "Let's talk about it after school today."

"*After school?* I can't, Mrs. Henley. I got basketball tryouts."

"You got bigger things to worry about than basketball right now," she warned. "I'll look for you after school today. We can talk more then."

"But Mrs. Henley—"

"Lionel, that's enough! You can either see me after school, or you can go straight to Ms. Spencer's office and talk to her about it right now," she said.

Lionel turned his back on her and stormed out of the classroom. She could say all she wanted, but there was no way she'd keep him from basketball. No way.

* * *

Lionel went straight to the gym after his last class.

Coach Barber and two other men were there, each with clipboards in hand. One man with the body of a weightlifter introduced himself as Coach Tubbs and directed the boys into the locker room to get changed.

Inside, Lionel walked into a crowded

maze of steel lockers that stretched in rows over the dirty tile floor. Wooden benches divided the rows of lockers. The air was a soupy mix of sweat, foot odor, and deodorant spray.

"Man, which one of you forgot to take a shower?" one boy complained.

"That's nasty," another said. "Someone open a window up in here."

Others were quiet and nervous as they changed, not saying a word to anyone, lost in their private thoughts. Lionel threw on the clothes he brought from home, eager to get onto the court.

"You played on Greene Street?" said a kid two inches taller than Lionel. He eyed Lionel's shirt and then his face. "Hey, ain't you the one who played Steve Morris last week?"

"Yeah, that's me," Lionel replied.

"Cool. My cousin played for Tanner Street this summer. He wasn't too happy 'cause of you," he said with a nod. "My name's Keith."

"Wassup. I'm Lionel," he said, bumping fists as they walked out onto the court. Lionel noticed a handful of students had come to watch. One of them was Tasha, who was perched on the lowest row of the bleachers closest to the courts. Lionel could see the bluish glow of her cell phone in her hands. Next to her sat Cooper and Desmond. Just behind them was Malika. She'd come to watch him!

An extra jolt of adrenaline shot through Lionel's chest. Up ahead, he spotted Steve Morris surrounded by a number of older kids Lionel didn't recognize.

"Hope y'all got your cameras today," Steve joked, bumping fists with the tallest kid Lionel had ever seen at Bluford, a muscular boy easily six-foot-six. He stood shoulders above everyone else.

"Who's that?" Lionel asked Keith.

"That's Okam Jeffers. He's Bluford's center. Dude is no joke," Keith said.

Suddenly, the whistle blew, and Coach Barber was talking, welcoming them, asking them to show respect and good sportsmanship.

"Not all of you will make the team today. Don't be discouraged. Even Michael Jordan failed to make the varsity team his first year. He learned from that and became the best player of all time," the coach continued.

"But I'm making the team," Lionel thought.

"What I want to see today is hustle. Focus. Effort. Now good luck!"

After making everyone stretch, the coaches split them into two groups. Then they started with practice drills. For the first one, each of the two groups lined up on opposite ends of the court and counted off so each player had a number. Lionel was number 9. Coach Barber then placed a single basketball on the ground at mid-court, and yelled out a number. The two players with that number had to sprint to the middle of court, try to grab the ball, and return to their basket to score. The other player had to stop them.

Lionel's neck throbbed as he waited for his number to be called.

"Nine!"

His shoes squeaked in protest as he exploded onto the court, accelerating so that he nearly collided with the kid on the other side. He reached mid-court first, but the other guy, one of Steve's friends, stripped him of the ball and started dribbling down court.

"Hustle! Hustle!" the coaches urged.

Lionel sprinted alongside his opponent as he went for the lay-up. As soon as he left the ground, Lionel struck.

Whap!

He knocked the ball from his opponent's shooting hand, cut behind him, and scooped it up, sprinting full speed back to his basket. His lay-up was in before the kid even got to his foul line.

Next the coaches made each group perform a shoot-around drill just like the ones Coach Hodden used over the summer. Lionel was full of so much energy, his first two shots were too strong, clanging off the rim loudly.

"Watch your form," Coach Tubbs barked.

But as Lionel continued, he found the zone. He became looser, and the hoop seemed to grow wider, easier to hit. He ended up sinking five of seven in an arch around the basket. He noticed the coaches taking notes. Most kids in his group made fewer than him, except for Keith, who tied him.

Coach Barber ran the third activity, a tough rebound drill that started with each player having to bounce the basketball off the backboard. Then they'd grab their own rebound, zip a quick pass to their coach, race down the court, catch a pass from their coach and try to make a lay-up.

Lionel watched as the drill exposed flaws in everyone's game. Some missed their rebounds and had to chase them awkwardly, slowing the rest of the line down. Others seemed to jog when they should run.

"C'mon, move!" Coach Tubbs barked. "Your opponents aren't gonna take their time. You gotta move!"

One kid didn't position his body right to catch the pass and was unable to shoot his lay-up until it was too late. His shot hit the underside of the backboard and bounced all the way to the bleachers. He looked embarrassed as he chased it down.

Lionel watched him run by. He felt the same way in Mrs. Henley's class.

"That boy don't belong out here!" someone said, while a few others laughed.

"Man, leave him alone!" Keith barked. "At least he's trying."

"That's right. That's right. We buildin' a team now," Coach Tubbs said, nodding encouragingly at Keith.

Then it was Lionel's turn. He banged the shot off the backboard and jumped up, snagging the rebound and whipping the pass at his coach. Lionel heard his shoes chirp on the floor as he pivoted around and sprinted down the court.

He'd watched the previous players and knew where the pass would be. He even figured out the best lane to travel, one that would give his shot the best angle.

And there it was, just as he expected. The pass rocketing in. His feet perfectly coordinated. He came off the ground, the ball curving off his fingers. A perfect lay-up, the best of his group.

"All right! All right!" Coach Tubbs said, pumping his fist. "That's what we're looking for!"

After two defensive drills, the coaches decided to end tryouts with some quick full-court games. For this final activity, the coaches selected teams. Lionel noticed that Coach Tubbs and Barber chatted for a few minutes, and then chose Keith and Lionel to be part of a team that was going against several var-sity guys, including Steve and Okam. The rest of the students sat on the side-lines, watching intently as if they knew the matchup was important.

Keith played center and lost the jump ball against Okam, who was much taller. Within seconds, Steve snagged the ball, and began racing down the court, his arm pumping like a piston as he dribbled.

Shoes squeaked against the hardwood. The ball smacked against the court like a drumbeat getting louder as Steve approached. Lionel immediately slid into Steve's path, his arms out, adjusting as Steve charged his way. If they were on the blacktop, Lionel figured Steve would have plowed through him like a freight train, but with the coaches there, Steve would be called for charging. Lionel knew he wouldn't let that happen.

Lionel watched Steve's eyes, saw him sizing him up. He wanted to steal the ball, but if he missed, Steve would have an easy basket. Instead Lionel stayed with him, sticking on Steve like glue, containing him as best he could. Steve dribbled fast, threw a double crossover, and nearly spun him off twice before Lionel finally stopped him just beyond the three-point line.

But then Steve began to roll to his right. Lionel moved to follow him and then saw a wall in front of him. It was Okam.

Crunch!

They collided, and Okam held him just enough for Steve to sneak by. A classic pick and roll. Lionel knew Steve was going for the basket. He darted toward the rim then, hoping to get the rebound from Steve's shot, but it was too late.

Wham!

Steve popped up and dunked the ball right over Keith. A perfect move. Lionel knew the two older boys had an edge because they had played together. They knew each other's game. It almost wasn't fair.

"Nice pick, Okam!" shouted a coach.

Lionel took the ball in to play then, going the other way, eyeing his teammates as he stormed down the court, seeing where they positioned themselves, figuring out how they were guarded.

Steve came at him just as he crossed the half court line. He shifted left, then right, trying to make Steve commit, but this time the crossover didn't work. Steve read it and trapped him without a shot. But then Keith came near. Lionel liked his instinct. He had game.

Lionel whipped a pass over to him and dashed inside. Keith saw his move and snaked an impossible bounce pass right back. Lionel scooped it up, but Okam, Bluford's big man, was right there, smothering him. His long arms seemed to be everywhere.

"Watch out for him, Okam," Steve warned. "He's quick!"

Okam was so close that Lionel could smell his sweat and see the trace of a mustache under his nose and a tiny scar beneath his chin.

"You ain't got nothin'," Okam grunted. "This is *my* house."

Lionel raised the ball fast with his hands, exaggerating his shoulder movement, as if he was about to take a big jump shot. Okam took the bait, jumping to block Lionel's shot, which never came.

Gotcha! Lionel thought, watching Okam fall for his fake, opening his lane to the basket.

And then it was all slow motion, like something out of a dream, the adrenaline surging, the anger at the past weeks transformed into power. Lionel's feet were moving, his pulse pounding, his body rising, his arm reaching higher than ever.

Whoomp!

Lionel's first dunk exploded like a bomb blast in the gym. Hoots and cheers erupted, and Keith slapped his hand. The rage that consumed him hours earlier seemed to lose its grip, unable to hold him down.

The whistle blew, and Coach Barber substituted in new players, but not before he yelled out words that echoed in Lionel's heart.

"Good, smart play. Way to hustle!"

Lionel's heart thundered as he sat down on the edge of the court, confident he'd made the team. But then his eye caught several people entering the back of the gym. Mr. Coleman, his study skills teacher, was there. So was Mrs. Henley and Ms. Spencer. Their eyes were locked on him.

Chapter 9

Lionel felt his stomach churn as Ms. Spencer pulled Coach Barber aside. His other teachers moved in close too, as if it was football and they were huddling.

"What are they doing here?" Keith asked.

"Someone's gettin' busted, that's what," another player answered.

Lionel stood up, his ears ringing, his heart knocking against his ribs. What were they saying?

Coach Tubbs continued running practice, while the small group of adults talked. After several seconds, Coach Barber winced as if he'd heard something that pained him. Then they all turned toward Lionel. Coach Barber called him over.

Lionel knew the other students were

watching as he forced himself to walk to the back corner of the gym.

"I'm sorry, son," Coach Barber said. "You get yourself straightened out, get your grades up, and I got a team that could use you."

It was a nightmare come true. Lionel shook at the words, tried to push them back, deny them.

"Huh?! What are you saying?"

"I hate to say this, but you're not eligible to join the team right now. Your grades—"

"No! You can't do that!" Lionel cried, his voice booming into the gym. "That ain't right! I was good out there, Coach!"

"C'mon everyone. There's nothin' to stare at. Get back to work," Coach Tubbs yelled in the distance. Lionel glanced back to see Desmond and Cooper leaning forward trying to listen to them. Malika held her chin, her mouth open as if she was watching an accident happen right before her eyes. Tasha was craning toward him too, her camera phone pointed right at him.

"I'm sorry, Lionel. But this isn't about the court. Grades and your conduct off the court are just as important," Ms. Spencer spoke up then. His teachers nodded in agreement.

"Don't do this!" Lionel begged, desperate to change their minds. His hands trembled, and his eyes started to sting. It felt as if they'd ganged up on him, robbing him right there in the middle of the gym for everyone to see, stealing the one thing that kept him from spinning out of control.

"You did it to yourself, and you can fix it yourself," Ms. Spencer added firmly. There was a note of sadness in her voice too, though Lionel didn't care. "Let's talk about it in my office. C'mon, Lionel." She gestured toward the doorway leading out of the gym. Lionel glanced back at the basketball court and the small crowd of people still watching him.

"Get those grades up, and come back to me," Coach Barber said then, putting a hand on Lionel's shoulder. "You're a smart and talented player. I wanna see you on the team."

Lionel shrugged his hand off as if the touch burned him.

"Don't take this from me," Lionel said to all of them, unable to express why basketball was so important. "It's all I got. Don't take it."

But in Ms. Spencer's office, they didn't

seem to understand.

"Lionel, you need a *C* average to play," Ms. Spencer explained as his other teachers looked on. "Everyone who plays for Bluford is under the same rules. That means you too."

"A *C* average?!" Lionel gasped. It was the final nail in the coffin.

"And you can start by handing in the work you owe in all your other classes," Ms. Spencer added.

Lionel rose from his chair then, a cold numbness spreading into his chest.

"I can't do the work," he said then, making eye contact with each of them one last time. "Do you understand that? I can't do it."

"What do you mean?" Mrs. Henley asked, her voice changing as if she'd just discovered something new, but Lionel didn't answer. He opened the door and walked out.

"Where are you going?" Ms. Spencer asked, following him into the hallway. "Lionel?"

Lionel kept moving, shutting out their voices and pushing their faces from his mind. He walked down the mostly empty hall and kicked open the front doors of Bluford High.

Deep inside him, a flame had been snuffed out. A dream had died.

* * *

Lionel ran from Bluford as fast as his feet would carry him. He sprinted past SuperFoods, weaved around a small crowd of teenagers and crossed in front of a car that skidded to avoid him. The driver cursed as he passed, and some of the kids cackled in laughter.

"Man, that boy don't look good," said one of them.

"Where's the fire, bro? Whatchu runnin' from?" said another.

Lionel felt as if he was on fire, as if flames were on him, consuming him, breaking him down until there was nothing left but ash and pain.

His feet carried him up a familiar block, pushing him to do one last thing before Bluford High School slipped away completely. He went two blocks north to Union Street and was suddenly dashing up the steps of Dontrell's house. A second later, he was knocking on the door.

Dontrell pulled the door open and looked at him, a strange expression on his face. Lionel cut him off before he could say a word.

"Yo, Trell. I'm sorry about what I said today in Mrs. Henley's class. That wasn't right," he said, reaching a fist out to his old friend.

Dontrell stood motionless, studying him. "You all right, L?" he asked. "Your eyes are all red."

Lionel nodded. "I just needed to apologize, you know? It ain't right that I teased you for doin' your work. Like you said, you was just tryin' to get by. Ain't no one should get on your case for that, especially not me."

Dontrell bumped his fist, and Lionel felt like it was done. He said his final goodbye. He turned and walked down the steps as he had for years. Only now it felt different, as if the world had changed somehow, and they'd never be the same.

"What happened at tryouts?" Dontrell asked. "You made the team, right?"

Lionel paused for a second unable to respond. "Talk to Tasha. She got it all," he said, imagining the rest of the school going online so they could see him screaming at his teachers in the gym. "I gotta go, Trell," he added. "Take care of yourself, bro."

Dontrell asked him something then, but Lionel tuned him out. He knew what he had to do next.

Back at home, Aunt Mimi confronted Lionel as soon as he walked in the door.

"Boy, where have you been?" she yelled. "Your principal called twice this afternoon. She wants your dad to come in for a conference right away. I told them he was on the road, but she asked for his cell number, and when I gave it her, she practically hung up on me. What happened?"

Lionel looked her in the eye. There was no point lying anymore. Dad probably knew everything by now. With Ms. Spencer's phone call, he'd know that Lionel lied about school, faked his signature, and didn't do his homework. He'd be furious. Maybe he'd even drive back to punish him.

Lionel could picture Dad's face, the veins in his neck bulging as he yelled, his eyes full of anger and disappointment. Dad would ground him and take away basketball and his job at the car wash. Then he'd go back to work, to Denise or whatever and Lionel would be alone again, failing school and trapped in the house. There was no way he could live like that.

"I quit school," he hissed.

"What?!" Aunt Mimi yelled, shaking her head as if she couldn't believe what she'd just heard. "You can't do that."

"I just did," he snapped, grabbing a trash bag and running down the hall to his bedroom with her right behind him. Kendra followed them and stood quietly at the edge of the hallway listening to everything.

"What are you doing?" his aunt asked, standing in his doorway with her hands on her hips.

Lionel rifled through his drawers, throwing his clothes into the bag.

"Packing."

"What do you mean, *packing?* Where you goin'?"

"My friend's house. I'm moving out," Lionel said, grabbing the small wad of cash he'd saved from the car wash.

Aunt Mimi looked as if she'd been slapped in the face. "Lionel, I don't know what's going on, but I can't let you leave. You're stayin' right here."

In the distance, Lionel heard Sahara cry. Aunt Mimi rolled her eyes in frustration. "Just a minute, baby," she yelled, yanking the plastic bag from his hands.

Lionel pulled the bag back, anger flaring in his chest.

"You can't keep me here. I ain't gotta listen to you!" he screamed, unable to stop the rage from boiling from his lips. "You ain't my momma!"

His aunt stepped back and let go of his bag, as if it stung her hands. He knew he'd hurt her feelings. He could see it on her face, and he wished he could take back the words. But it was too late.

"Don't you *ever* talk to me like that!" she yelled. "I work too hard around here for that." Sahara's cries grew louder, and Aunt Mimi turned without a word and raced back down the hallway after her. For a second, the room was quiet.

"Don't leave, Lionel," Kendra begged. Her voice felt like a knife digging into Lionel's stomach. "Please. I don't want you to go."

Lionel forced himself to keep moving, stuffing his trash bag with the last of his belongings.

"It ain't right," she continued. "First Momma. Then Daddy. Now you. What am I supposed to do? I don't wanna be here alone. It's not even home anymore."

Lionel shook his head. His sister's

117

words held him for a second, anchoring him to the floor. But there at the edge of his bed was the notebook from the other day, his drawing still visible. He could see the championship banner he'd sketched for Mrs. Henley's assignment, his words scribbled underneath.

Lionel's dreem.

It was an insult, a reminder of the door Ms. Spencer had slammed shut on him just an hour ago. And yet it also pointed to what would happen if he stayed in the house. It would be more failure at school, more punishment too. No work. No basketball, not at Bluford or anywhere. And all the while, he'd know Dad was hiding Denise under his nose. It was as if the walls were a prison trying to close in on him. He had to escape.

Lionel leaned forward and put his arms around his little sister. She sobbed quietly, and he knew she'd figured out what was happening next.

"I'm sorry, but I gotta do this," he said then, hugging her tight. "You'll be all right. And if you ever need me, I'll be at Jamar's house on 43rd Street. He works with me at the car wash."

Without another word, he ran down

the hallway and out the front door. Ms. Walker was sweeping her stoop and watched as Lionel rushed from his house carrying his bag.

"Where you goin' in such a hurry?"

Lionel didn't even look at her, but a voice behind him answered her question.

"He's quittin' school and runnin' away, that's what he's doin'." His aunt had followed him out, holding Sahara in her arms.

"Quittin' school?!" Ms. Walker barked. "Boy, you got any sense in that brain of yours?"

Lionel ignored her. He was about to pass her stoop when she came hurrying down her steps, nearly colliding with him.

"Look at me when I'm talking to you!" she commanded.

Lionel was stunned. He'd never heard her speak to anyone this way.

"You listen to me. If you quit school, you'll throw everything away. All that your mother and father been fighting for all these years," she said.

"Ms. Walker. You don't understand—"

"What don't I understand? I been walking this earth a lot longer than you, and I'll tell you something. You quit now, and it ain't gonna get easier. How you gonna get a good job without an education? Huh? Who's gonna hire you?"

Lionel shrugged. He wasn't thinking about a job or tomorrow. He just wanted her to stop, so he could leave Cypress Street once and for all. But she kept on going, getting louder each second.

"You'll just be another kid with no skills, no idea who he is or how much he's missing out on. How you gonna get far like that?"

Lionel shifted the heavy trash bag to his other shoulder, trying to avoid her eyes.

"There's a whole world out there for you to see," she continued. "But you gotta finish school so you can rise up to it. Too many good kids today never do. Instead they're out there on the corner or strung out or worse, and I'm tired of it," she yelled. "You're better than that! You hear me?"

A speeding police car raced through the intersection up ahead, its flashing lights reflected in Ms. Walker's glasses like red and blue flames.

"I gotta go."

She grabbed his arm, her hand like a

claw on his bicep.

"No one owes you anything, Lionel. You gotta work for it. You gotta earn it, just like in basketball. Now I know you're smart. My Russell was smart too, and he got his chance taken from him. You still got yours. Don't go throwin' it away. You hear me?!"

Lionel cringed at her words. It was as if she'd draped Russell's ghost on his shoulders for him to carry. Her eyes stayed focused on him as if she was trying to drill into him with her stare. He could barely look at them, though he saw they were glistening and swollen. He could read the pain in them more easily than any words, and he felt it too. But she didn't understand that he'd failed school, that it was no longer an option for him. The doors were closed.

As soon as her grip relaxed, Lionel started walking.

"No! Don't go," his sister screamed, but Lionel blocked it out.

He headed straight to his new home: Jamar's house.

Chapter 10

Lionel's arms were sore by the time he reached Jamar's block. The last of the daylight had died away as he crept through the broken gate, dropped his clothes on the step, and knocked on the door. Overhead a police helicopter chopped at the sky.

"What up, L!" Jamar said, beaming at him as he opened the door. "You finally made up your mind?"

Lionel immediately smelled the pungent odor of marijuana, and he could see that Jamar's eyes were pink and blood-shot. The scent made him pause at the doorway. For a half second, he felt as if he was on the court, looking for his options.

Pass. Dribble. Shoot.

But now Lionel knew he had no other

choices. Jamar's place was his only move.

"Yeah," Lionel said, stepping inside, feeling the smoky air spill over him.

"Cool!" Jamar said, slapping his hand. "Put your stuff in the room and make yourself at home. This your crib now."

"Thanks," Lionel said, scanning the cluttered living room. Everything was the same as Lionel remembered it, except that a ripped brown recliner was now next to the sagging green couch. And several cases of beer were stacked next to a cooler in the far corner of the room.

"You picked a good night to come over," Jamar said, glancing over at the alcohol. "My cousin's having a bunch of his friends over. Should be here soon."

Lionel felt uneasy as he carried his bag into the messy bedroom. The air inside was thick and close, smelling like a soupy mixture of marijuana smoke, old tires, and the wax they used at the car wash. Jamar quickly kicked all his things aside, clearing half the floor for Lionel.

"You want a hit?" he said, offering Lionel what looked like a half smoked cigar. "You look like you could use it."

"No thanks, Jamar," Lionel said,

squirming inside. Even though he was free of his father, he couldn't just let go of the rules he'd lived by for so long. He'd always been clean, an athlete for the Police Athletic League, the son of two parents who warned him about drugs and alcohol. And yet now, he felt smoke seeping onto his clothes, coating his hair and skin, sinking into his lungs.

"So why'd you decide to move in?" Jamar asked. "I thought Felix scared you."

"I quit school today," Lionel admitted. "They won't let me join the basketball team, so why should I stay there?"

"That's what I was trying to tell you!" Jamar said with an approving nod. "Let me guess. You was failing, right?"

The question made Lionel wince. He couldn't deny the truth. He *was* failing. There was no sense in keeping secrets. But somehow telling Jamar bothered him. It was like admitting defeat and accepting what he'd fought against for so long, that he was too stupid for school.

"Yeah, so what?" he replied finally, hating the words as they dropped off his tongue.

"You just like me," Jamar said,

glancing over at the old picture of his mother at his bedside. "After my mom got sick, I had no time for school. My teachers started failin' me, so I quit."

"What happened to her?" Lionel couldn't stop himself from asking.

"I told you, she got sick," Jamar said, fiddling with a pack of matches. "She always talked about liking school too, but it didn't help her."

Lionel unpacked his clothes, pretending not to hear the sadness in Jamar's voice, even as it spread into the cramped bedroom like more smoke.

Just then, Lionel heard car doors slam shut outside. A second later, the front door opened and laughter poured into the hallway.

"Sounds like Andre and his friends are here," Jamar said. "C'mon."

Lionel felt a wave of dizziness as he walked with Jamar back to the living room. Suddenly a hip-hop beat cracked and pulsed through the small house.

Maybe it was the smoke and the noise or his own weariness from tryouts, but Lionel felt his own head getting hazy. He wobbled slightly as he followed Jamar into the living room. Andre and four other people he'd never met before stood around the cooler. Two of them were girls. All of them seemed to be a few years older than Jamar, who was seventeen.

"Check it out, Andre. Lionel's gonna live with us," Jamar explained.

"He got rent money?" Andre asked as three more people came in the front door.

"Yeah, he's cool, right Lionel?"

Lionel nodded as Jamar handed him a bottle of beer.

"No thanks," Lionel said.

"C'mon, man. You're free now," Jamar urged. "You ain't gotta worry. No one's gonna go telling your dad or anything."

Lionel took the cold bottle in his hand as the music continued to pound in his head. On the couch at the far side of the room, Lionel saw two people light up a joint. Nearby Andre and a friend gulped beer and talked with the girls who laughed loudly. One of them wore a snug jean skirt and stumbled into Andre as she talked.

"That's Aisha, Andre's girlfriend. She's drunk already, as usual," laughed Jamar.

The dizziness in Lionel's head was spreading. His hands tingled, and his feet felt strangely unsteady. Smoke tickled the back of his throat, making him cough every few minutes. Reluctantly, he took a gulp of beer to help. At first, the taste was horrible, and he nearly gagged. But with the music pumping, the growing haze in his brain, and the thirst and itch of his throat, it gradually bothered him less.

"I shouldn't be doin' this," he said flatly at one point, looking at the bottle in his hand, feeling the smoke sting his eyes. He was sitting in a corner of the living room, watching everyone else laugh and talk around him.

"Man, you get used to it," Jamar answered. "Helps you stop thinkin', you know?"

Soon Jamar was handing him a second beer and then a third as the smoke and music mixed and swirled in the air. Already his anger at Bluford and Dad had lost its edge. School was a fading memory slipping behind him forever, dissolving in the mind-numbing haze.

Even Malika's pretty face seemed foggy when he pictured it, along with Dontrell and everyone else at Bluford. He almost couldn't feel the sadness of leaving them all behind, of dropping out of their world, a world that was once his.

Lionel had lost count of how much he'd drunk when he realized Jamar was gone.

Nearby a few people were dancing. Their moving bodies made Lionel's dizziness worsen, so he decided to go to his room to escape. But several people were in the bedroom sitting on the mattress talking quietly with Jamar.

"Hey, there's my new roommate," he said, but Lionel turned away at the blast of smoke that hit him.

He rushed back to the living room where Aisha danced into him, nearly falling over. Lionel caught her and held her up, and she looked at him, her eyes glassy, her hands on his shoulders.

"Sorry," she said with a drunken smile.

Then someone started yelling.

"Are you touching my girl?!"

The voice was vaguely familiar, but it seemed far away and foggy, aimed at someone else, Lionel thought.

And then Andre was in his face, screaming at him. Lionel was in a cloud of his breath and spit.

"I'ma beat you down right here if you touch her again. You hear me?"

"It's cool. I was just helping her,"

Lionel explained, putting his hands up, but the room was spinning now, and a sour taste began to gather in his mouth.

Lost in the haze and smoke and music, Lionel staggered to the bathroom as his stomach began to heave. Blurred and groggy, Lionel stumbled to the toilet as beer-tinged vomit began spilling golden and sour down his shirt and splashing onto the back of the toilet. He heard the scream of girls and the cackle of laughter as someone opened the door on him.

"That boy is a lightweight."

"Ew, that's nasty!"

"Gross!"

Lionel slammed the door shut and fell to his hands and knees, hunched over the toilet. Staring down at his reflection in the fluids from his stomach, Lionel saw himself for what he was.

Stupid. Failure. Dropout. The words erupted from deep inside, mocking him.

He hated what he saw, but he knew it was his fault. He'd made himself into the mess that returned his gaze. Strangely, then, the words of Langston Hughes's poem came back to him, like the voice from a distant past.

What happens to a dream deferred?

Does it dry up
like a raisin in the sun?
Or fester like a sore—
And then run?
Does it stink like rotten meat?
Or crust and sugar over—
like a syrupy sweet?
Maybe it just sags
like a heavy load.

Or does it explode?

For the first time, Lionel knew the answers to the questions in the poem. A dream does all those things if it isn't lived, he realized. It dries up, rots, stinks, explodes. But it does something else too. It dies.

Looking at his reflection in the stinking fluid, Lionel knew he couldn't stay with Jamar. If he did, he would end up just like him, working at a meaningless job, pretending to be happy as he numbed himself each day. There would be no school, but there'd also be no basketball, no family, no future. Lionel didn't want that. He forced himself off the floor. He knew he had to get out of the house now or he'd never make it.

Lionel staggered through the crowd and stumbled to the door, his head pounding in pain, his stomach threatening to retch with each step. His balance still wasn't right, and he tripped through the broken gate, nearly twisting his ankle as he emerged onto the street. After just half a block, Lionel had to vomit again, holding himself against a wall as he spit out the last contents of his stomach, trying to keep his good shoes clean. His head felt as if someone was trying to hammer huge nails into his skull.

A block further, with his head aching and dizzy, Lionel felt lost. In the haze of smoke and drink, the dark unfamiliar neighborhood was like a maze, the houses strange and ominous. Was he still on 43rd Street? Was there someone he could ask for directions? Should he just go back to Jamar's house? What time was it? He had no idea.

Just then, Lionel heard a thundering beat coming up the block from behind him. He waited for the car to drive by and the music to fade, but that didn't happen. Instead it held steady, cracking and thumping the air behind him, but never passing, the words loud and clear.

This ain't no game.
  This is fo' real
You gonna get hurt,
  them cuts won't heal
You gonna get stabbed,
  that blood's gonna spill
You gonna cry out
  before you get killed.

Lionel knew the car was following him then. He knew he couldn't be that far from Jamar's, but he also knew he was too dizzy and sick to run. He thought of Russell and what Ms. Walker had said to him.

"My Russell had his chance taken from him. Don't you waste yours."

The music cut off abruptly and Lionel could hear the engine humming, the tires rolling slowly on the asphalt, the squeak of brakes.

"Yo, where you from? I don't know you," shouted a voice.

Lionel kept walking, pretending not to hear.

"I'm talking to you! Where you goin'?"

Lionel peeked to his left and saw the car, a dark blue sedan. Along with the driver, three other guys were inside, all of them watching him. The one yelling at him was in the passenger seat, a reverse bandanna on his forehead. Lionel knew he needed to give them an answer.

"I'm just goin' home man," Lionel said. "I don't want no trouble."

"Too late for that."

All four car doors opened then, and Lionel watched as the guys surrounded him. His heart pounded in his aching skull. The world spun around him, and he could barely stand, let alone run.

"Please," he said, thinking of Russell. Was this the way he spent his last minutes? Was this how his life ended that afternoon two years ago?

Crunch!

Suddenly fists were punching him, and he was on the ground. A kick landed in the ribs, and Lionel gasped for air, the pain shooting into him like a hot knife. Lionel's mind raced to his father. He pictured Dad hearing the news that his son died right there on the sidewalk like so many other kids in the neighborhood.

"I'm sorry, Dad," Lionel thought. *"I never wanted it to end up like this."*

Lionel felt hands yank from his pocket the money he'd grabbed earlier. Then his expensive Nikes were pulled off as he rolled on the ground in pain.

"You stupid to walk out here like this," hissed one of the guys standing over him.

The world grew hazier, and Lionel heard Reverend Simmons's words echo in his mind.

"And yet this son is not lost. None of us are."

That's when he noticed twin beams of light shining down the street and heard the sound of a truck thundering through the darkness.

Then there was a blur of hurried voices. Feet scampering. A car racing off, its tires screeching against the asphalt. The grumble of an enormous diesel engine growing closer. The image of his father's face dissolving.

"Lionel, talk to me! Talk to me, son! Lionel!"

Lionel felt as if he was falling, the world going cold and dark.

* * *

Lionel woke up in a strange bed, wincing at the bright morning sun that filled his room with light. He tried to sit up, but his head throbbed and pain

134

ripped into his side, making him groan.

"Stay still, son. You're in the hospital," a familiar voice said. "Your ribs are bruised."

He glanced up to see his father sitting at his bedside, his face lined with worry, his eyes tired and bloodshot. He looked as if he hadn't slept in days.

"How you feeling?" he asked, putting a hand on Lionel's shoulder.

Lionel turned away. A wave of guilt swept over him.

"Dad, I'm sorry. I never meant for this to happen," he replied. He expected his father to be furious and lecture him on everything he'd done wrong, but instead Dad reached over and hugged him.

"You scared me, Lionel," he said, his voice cracking. "Thank God your principal called and your sister knew where you were. I don't know what I'd do if something happened to you."

Lionel cringed. Dad's voice made him feel even more dishonest. He needed to tell his father the truth, but the words stuck in his throat. He felt like a blister about to burst.

"Dad, I got problems," he said finally. "I ain't been tellin' you 'cause I knew you'd get mad, but I don't know what to do." The words erupted from him then. He described everything that had happened at Bluford, the forged letter, even the events at Jamar's and his decision to quit school.

"I messed up, Dad. I'm sorry. I just didn't want you to know. I'm the dumbest kid in my class," he admitted, certain his father would punish him.

"You're *not* dumb, Lionel," Dad snapped. "I don't want to ever hear you say that. You're smart, too smart sometimes, from what your principal told me today. But you need some extra work on your reading skills. I know somethin' about that," Dad said.

"Huh?"

"I never graduated high school," Dad declared.

Lionel turned so quickly his ribs hurt. "You serious?"

"That's right. I was a little older than you when I got tired of people making fun of me in school, calling me slow or whatever. So one day I quit. It was the biggest mistake of my life. Your mom and I kept it a secret 'cause we didn't want you following in my footsteps. Why else you think I'm always on your case? I don't want you to have to come up like me, working like a dog and needing every cent just to get by. If I had a better job, maybe your momma would be here with us instead of overseas right now," he said bitterly.

Lionel's head was spinning. But Dad kept talking, the most they'd spoken in years.

"I'm trying to fix my mistake by getting my GED. I started studying about a month ago, so I can get a promotion and be home more for you and your sister. If I pass all my tests, I'll have my high school diploma in about six weeks. That's why I've been away so much lately. All because I dropped out."

Lionel heard everything Dad said, but one phrase stuck in his mind. *Away so much lately.* Ever since he talked to Kendra, Lionel had his own ideas where Dad was each week. Suddenly the question was racing off his tongue.

"What about Denise?" Lionel blurted. "You still got time to see her."

His father winced and shook his head. "I have to see her, Lionel. She's my tutor. One of your mom's army people put us in touch. I see her every Friday. She's been helping me work on my skills, just like you gotta work on yours. I didn't tell you 'cause I was embarrassed. But after talking with Mrs. Henley and Ms. Spencer, I knew you needed to hear the truth from me."

"Your *tutor*?!" Lionel's jaw dropped as Dad's words sunk in. Part of him was relieved to hear the truth, but another part was angry that he'd hidden it for so long. "You should have told us!"

"You're right, Lionel," Dad agreed. "But I didn't want you to know I was getting help. You see, you and me, we're the same. Except you got a choice to do things right the *first* time around—and you're better at basketball than I ever was."

"Yeah, well that don't matter 'cause they won't let me play."

"Listen to me. Ms. Spencer and I got to talking," Dad explained. "She told me about a bunch of programs at Bluford to help with school. You do your work, and you'll get on that basketball team. But you gotta come home and get back in school first. You hear me?"

Lionel struggled to grasp what he'd just learned. It was as if the world was shifting somehow. Doors that had been shut against him were now ready to be opened again.

"I don't know if I can do it, Dad,"

Lionel admitted. "I ain't never been good at school."

"You were never able to dunk before neither, right? But you can now," Dad said.

Lionel smiled. His dad had a point, one Lionel would cling to in the months ahead.

Just then, a nurse stepped into the room and looked at the chart at Lionel's feet.

"How we doin' this morning?" she asked, inspecting his bandages and his eyes.

"We're good," Lionel said, glancing over at his father and thinking about the events of the past few weeks. He had been lost. He'd walked a downward spiral and barely escaped. He could feel the scars inside and out. And yet he was still standing.

Bluford High School would still be an enormous challenge. Reading would intimidate him. Kids would tease him. Some might call him stupid, or worse. But he had his father on his side, along with a few teachers and an old coach. Dontrell would have his back. Maybe Malika would too. Perhaps they'd even grow into something more. After everything that happened, Lionel wanted to find out.

By some miracle, he'd been given something many people never get. A second shot. He planned to make it count.

* * *

Several weeks later, on a Saturday morning, two players stepped onto a blacktop court near Bluford High School. One was young and fast, explosively quick. The other was older, slower, and more cautious but with a decent outside shot. They joked and laughed as much as they played. And for the hour they were on the court, people gave them space, recognizing that they were part of the most sacred team of all. Family.